"Why are you here?" she asked.

Beckett stayed silent for a moment as Andie tried to come up with some reasons. Had he changed his mind about her? He glanced at the cast on her wrist. "I came to apologize," he said.

"For what?" For her injury? It hadn't been his fault. Or for pushing her away? When he didn't expand on his answer, she figured the flowers were a guilt offering. He didn't say anything further and she gave a short nod. "I need to get back to my class."

Andie started to walk inside when he called her name. She turned, and he reached for her free hand. "I'm not good with words like you are."

"What do you want, Beckett?"

"I want you to come back and work on the window with me..."

Dear Reader,

Six years ago, I met an army veteran who had fought in Iraq and Afghanistan. When I thanked him for his service, he got very angry. I asked him why he was so upset, and he answered that I didn't know what he'd had to do in order to survive. That he had lost more men from his squad to suicide than to combat. I never forgot him or his words, and my hero in this story, Beckett, is based on that brief encounter.

Like the man I met, Beckett suffers from PTSD, post-traumatic stress disorder. Beckett has tried everything to forget his time in the war, including alcohol, prescription drugs and therapy. He's about to meet a black Lab named Phoebe, a trained therapy dog, to help him cope, and a Vietnam war veteran named Russ, who knows how Beckett feels, since he was in the same frame of mind when he came home from war.

I hope that this story opens up conversations about mental health and our veterans. And to the man I met six years ago, I hope he has finally found peace.

Syndi

HEARTWARMING

Soldier of Her Heart

—

Syndi Powell

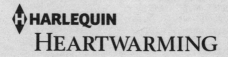

HARLEQUIN®
HEARTWARMING™

ISBN-13: 978-1-335-88960-7

Soldier of Her Heart

Recycling programs
for this product may
not exist in your area.

This edition published by arrangement with Harlequin Books S.A.

For questions and comments about the quality of this book,
please contact us at CustomerService@Harlequin.com.

Harlequin Enterprises ULC
22 Adelaide St. West, 40th Floor
Toronto, Ontario M5H 4E3, Canada
www.Harlequin.com

Printed in U.S.A.

Syndi Powell started writing stories when she was young and has made it a lifelong pursuit. She's been reading Harlequin romance novels since she was in her teens and is thrilled to be on the Harlequin team. She loves to connect with readers on Twitter, @syndipowell, or on her Facebook author page, Facebook.com/syndipowellauthor.

Books by Syndi Powell

Harlequin Heartwarming

Their Forever Home
Finding Her Family
Healing Hearts
Afraid to Lose Her
The Sweetheart Deal
Two-Part Harmony
Risk of Falling
The Reluctant Bachelor

Visit the Author Profile page
at Harlequin.com for more titles.

Dedicated to my grandfathers,
Robert Layher and Charles Hawkins,
who served in World War II, and my uncle,
Mike Hawkins, who served in Vietnam.

And also to the men and women in the
armed services who fight and sacrifice
so much for our freedoms.

Thank you, and welcome home.

CHAPTER ONE

"Boss, we've got a problem."

Beckett paused at the words, resting the sledgehammer he'd been using to tear up the kitchen's ceramic tile floor. "Rob, I hired you so that we wouldn't have problems. What's wrong?"

The younger man shook his head. "I think you need to see this."

Beckett followed him into the living room of the house they'd started to renovate that morning. He'd been buying places in Detroit neighborhoods, fixing them up and selling them for a profit. His business was still new, not quite two years old, but solid. Rob pointed at the east living room wall. "There's two walls."

"Two?" He approached the wall and peered into the foot-wide hole where Rob had taken down the drywall. Reaching for his cell phone from his back pocket, Beckett used the flashlight feature to try to examine what lay behind the outer wall.

Rob was right. There was a second plywood wall behind the first. Why in the world would someone lose square footage by building it six inches out from the original wall?

Beckett turned back to Rob. "That explains why the room dimensions were off from the blueprints."

"What are we going to do about it?"

"Nothing. For now." He wanted time to think about it first so they didn't act rashly. "Why don't you tackle the master bedroom walls for now. We'll revisit this wall later."

Rob gave a nod and left Beckett, who returned to the kitchen. He wanted to get this floor up before quitting for the day. He raised the sledgehammer over his head and brought it down on the ceramic. It felt good to break apart the tiles, straining his muscles as he hefted the hammer above his head again and again to smash it onto the floor. He found the demolition oddly satisfying when work on a house began.

Later, he hoped he would find the same appreciation when he handed the keys over to the new owners and deposited their check into his bank account. But for now, he'd revel at the burn in his biceps as he smashed the hammer back down onto the tiles.

After an hour, he stopped his work to wipe his forehead with an old bandanna he kept in the back pocket of his jeans. Rob popped his head into the room. "I'm taking off for the night and thought I'd join some buddies at the pub to celebrate the New Year. You in?"

Beckett put his bandanna back into his pocket, hoping it looked as if he was seriously considering the invitation, although he already knew his answer. After a moment, he shook his head. "I want to finish tearing up this floor tonight, then prime it for the new tiles."

Rob glanced at his watch. "It's already after seven. You planning on working all night?"

If he could, he would keep working on the house for days without sleeping. Because working made him stop thinking and kept him awake. Whereas sleeping only brought bad dreams. He gave Rob a shrug. "You go on. I'll see you bright and early tomorrow morning."

"Tomorrow is New Year's Day, and you gave me the day off." Rob frowned at him. "Are you okay, man?"

Beckett waved off his concern. "I'm fine. I just forgot what day it was. I'll see you after the holiday."

Rob peered at him briefly and then nodded. "Maybe you could use a night out with the guys. Come with us, Beckett. I'll even buy the first round of beers."

The thought of sitting in a bar with people all around him made his heart stutter. He swallowed the bile that rose in his throat. "Another time."

"I'm holding you to that."

Beckett agreed, but acknowledged to himself that it would never happen. He didn't go to loud public places like bars or restaurants. He'd put off Rob's invitations until the guy gave up on trying to include him. Beckett didn't see the need to be part of the group anymore because he was better off on his own.

He returned to scooping up the floor tiles with a dustpan and tossing them into an empty cardboard box that he had repurposed earlier. He needed to work. To stay busy. To keep his mind occupied and away from thoughts of the past.

His stomach growled as he finished collecting the last tiles. Glancing at his watch, he realized it was almost nine, and he'd eaten lunch more than eight hours ago. No wonder his belly felt as if it was gnawing on itself. He left the house to walk to his truck parked in the driveway, pulled out the cooler he kept stocked with food for times such as this and chose a salami sandwich. He returned to the warmth of the house and took a seat on an overturned plastic bucket. Unwrapping the sandwich, he took a large bite and glanced around the living room as he ate. The wall behind the wall bothered him. What if the second wall hid a structural issue? While his inspector had assured him that the house was sound, it could be hiding a surprise.

He put his half-eaten sandwich down on the bucket and retrieved his sledgehammer from the kitchen. He swung the hammer into the wall, letting pieces of plaster fall onto the wooden floor. He ripped off a piece of the wall and tossed it aside, then hefted the sledgehammer over his shoulder, bringing it down on the next section of the wall. After thirty minutes, he'd opened up most of the first wall.

To remove the rest—the framing—he'd need his saw. What in the world was this wall concealing? Anticipation of what he might discover pushed him to keep going.

With the framing now gone, he started to take down the inner wall even though his muscles protested at their continued use. But he couldn't stop now without finding out what secrets the house was concealing from him.

Once he'd gotten the wall down to the studs, he paused and stared at the stained glass window that had been revealed. He put a hand against the cool glass and wondered why anyone would ever cover up something so beautiful. They'd even bricked it over on the exterior of the house. True, the cracks in the glass gave it an eerie beauty, but it looked amazing all the same. The window measured at least two feet across and was four feet high, portraying a boat sailing by a lighthouse that sent out shards of light. Red and black glass squares bordered the window.

He took a step back. He didn't know anything about repairing windows much less stained glass. He fished his cell phone from a pocket and dialed up another friend in the contracting business. The call went to voice mail, so he waited for the beep. "Hey, Cassie. Beckett here. I just found a stained glass window in this house I'm flipping. Do you know anyone who might be able to repair it? I'd hate to tear it out and throw it in the trash. Call me."

He put away the phone and returned to his sandwich. Sitting again on the bucket, he stared at the window and wondered what it all meant. *I promise I'm going to find out.*

ANDIE LOWMAN SIPPED her glass of moscato and debated how much longer she had to stay at the New Year's Eve party that she'd been dragged to. She would much rather have been home wearing an oversize sweatshirt with leggings and sitting on her couch with the remote control in her hand to watch the ball drop in Times Square. She might be as social as the next woman, but after the past difficult year, she wanted to stay home and nurse her hurting heart. Instead, she had squeezed into a sequined dress and high heels and stood by herself looking around the crammed hall. Most of the crowd was paired off in couples, and she felt out of place in her singlehood. Even her sister, Cassie, had her fiancé, John, with her. She should have brought a friend with her, but most of them had plans with boyfriends or husbands. So here she sat, feeling like a third wheel to her sister's blossoming relationship.

Speaking of her sister, Cassie joined Andie at the table. "I think I have a job for you."

Andie rested her cheek against her fist. "I have a job. I work for Dr. Frazier's office." After her father's construction company had been shut down, she'd found a job answering phones for a popular oncologist. Maybe it wasn't her passion, but at least it paid the bills.

"This one would involve that fancy degree of yours. Interested?"

More than interested. She'd graduated more than a year before with her master's degree in art education. Unfortunately, most school districts had cut their budgets in the arts, which meant she hadn't found a teaching position. She still sent out résumés, hoping for a nibble. At this point, she'd take a part-time position. Anything to keep her teaching credentials current.

Andie sat up straight in the chair and peered at her sister. "Keep talking."

Cassie grinned in response and leaned in to be heard over the music. "Beckett, a friend of mine, just called and needs your expertise."

Andie frowned, pausing at those words. "My expertise?"

"With stained glass windows. He's looking for someone who knows how to repair them."

The bubble of excitement that had started in her belly popped with disappointment. "You know that my knowledge of stained glass is more on an academic level than a practical one, right? I might have created a few, but I've never repaired them."

"Don't sell yourself short. If anyone could do this, it would be you, Andie." Cassie cocked her head to the side. "Isn't that basically the same speech you gave me when I wasn't sure I could step into Daddy's shoes with the construction company? Maybe it didn't happen the way I expected with Daddy going to jail for embezzling, but you helped me find my confidence. Let me return the favor."

Andie sighed and tapped her fingers against the wineglass. It wouldn't hurt to at least look at the window, would it? Depending on the age and condition, she knew several glaziers who might be willing to repair it. "Fine. Text me his information, and I'll contact him tomorrow."

Cassie took out her cell phone and handed it to Andie. "Why not call him now?"

"You're pushy, you know?" Having nothing else to do on this night of beginnings, she accepted the phone and stood. "I'll take the call outside so I can actually hear him above the revelry."

Before she could leave the table, Cassie tugged on her wrist. "There's something you should know about Beckett." She paused for a long moment, then shook her head. "Never mind. You'll figure it out on your own."

With those cryptic words following her, Andie took her sister's cell phone outside to the patio where several tall heaters had been placed. She found Beckett's name in the call history and pressed his name before putting the phone to her ear. It rang only once before a gruff voice answered, "Beckett."

Okay, so that was not what she had expected. "Mr. Beckett, this is Andie Lowman. My sister, Cassie, said that you were looking for someone to repair a stained glass window."

"It's about time you called me back. I don't have all night to be waiting around for you to take care of this."

She frowned at his tone though she knew he couldn't see her. If her mother could hear how he was speaking, she would have lectured him on phone etiquette. As it was, Andie took a deep breath before continuing. "Why don't you first tell me what you're looking for?"

He slowed his words as if she couldn't comprehend English. "The window is broken. I want it fixed. Got it?"

"Yes, I understand that part, but—"

She heard him sigh on the other end. "That came out wrong. Sorry, it's been a weird day. I need an expert, and your sister must think highly of you to recommend you."

That was much better. "Thank you, Mr. Beckett."

"When can you get here?"

She thought of the empty space that filled her Saturday morning. "Would this weekend suffice?"

He made a rude noise on the other end of the phone. "What's wrong with now?"

She glanced at her wrist and noted the time. "Mr. Beckett, it's close to midnight on New Year's Eve. Considering the late hour and the festivities of this evening, Saturday morning would be more appropriate for me to assess your situation and give you the recommendations I might have for its reparation."

"Using big words doesn't impress me." He sighed on the other end. "Fine, 9 a.m. Saturday morning and not a minute later."

He gave her the address and hung up before she could say another word. She stared at her sister's cell phone and wondered what this Mr. Beckett would be like in person if this was the way he behaved over the phone.

She returned to the party to find that John had gotten her sister onto the dance floor while the band played an appropriately slow love song. Cassie's head rested on John's chest as he waltzed her around the room. Her tomboy sister had turned into a princess.

Part of Andie wished that she could meet a man like the one her sister had found. John was kind, funny and smart. And he was good-looking, but not vain about it. In fact, she didn't think he realized the effect he had on the opposite sex.

Maybe it was time to start putting herself out more into the world. To start expecting good things to happen. To make strides in finding her dream career. For years, she had been known as the one to fix things. If there was a delivery problem for one of her father's projects, she called around and found a solution. When a friend had problems with a boyfriend or job, Andie had the right advice for them to fix the issue. But when it came to her own life, she made things worse rather than better.

But that stopped now.

With it being only moments away from the New Year, perhaps she couldn't have found a better time to make some resolutions about her life. And maybe if she wished for a life filled with passion and love when the clock struck midnight, Cupid might be more than willing to help a girl out.

ANDIE HANDED THE appointment card across the receptionist desk to Mrs. Prentkowski. "We'll see you back in six months, Mrs. P. Hopefully it will be a lot warmer weather here in Michigan then."

Mrs. Prentkowski smiled and placed the card into her purse and left the doctor's office while Andie saved the appointment into Dr. Frazier's electronic calendar.

One of the nurses stopped at the desk and checked the appointment log before taking a seat on the corner of the desk. "I can't get this tablet to save the patient's info."

Andie took it from her, noticed that one of the fields had been locked on a default and changed the settings. She handed the tablet back to Stephanie. "All fixed."

Stephanie thanked her and sighed. "Remind me again why I thought private practice would be a better fit for me."

"Because you wanted a regular life after work rather than standing on your feet all hours of the day at the hospital." Andie looked up at her best friend in the office. "Really, Steph, you should be grateful to be here. Everyone wants to work with Dr. Frazier."

Stephanie huffed and pushed her bangs off to the side of her forehead. "You're right as always. It must be annoying to be you. Gorgeous. Talented. And always right."

If Andie had always been right, she would be using her artistic talents instead of answering phones and scheduling appointments. But she plastered a smile on to her face and nodded. "Yes. And you forgot annoying." She handed a file to Steph. "Dr. Frazier's two o'clock is waiting in the lobby."

"You're still going out with us tonight, right? You backed out on us last time, and I'm holding you to your promise of a rain check. No excuses."

Her sofa at home and the remote in her hand held a stronger pull on her evening than going out to a restaurant with her coworkers, but she had promised and Lowmans didn't break their word. Despite her father's recent incarceration for embezzling from his own company, she'd grown up being taught that the Lowman family had integrity. And she'd made that New Year's resolution to put herself more out into the world. To stop waiting for something to happen. She finally gave a short nod. "I'll be there."

Stephanie smiled and pushed herself off the desk. "Good. And I think you might actually have some fun. Maybe even meet that guy you wished for on New Year's."

Andie closed her eyes and tipped her head back, groaning. "Remind me not to tell you everything."

"Too late."

THE ATMOSPHERE AT the sports bar and grill was subdued, probably due to the many who had given up alcohol as part of their New Year's resolutions. Andie scanned the faces in the bar until she spotted Stephanie, who stood talking to a nurse in another of the offices in their complex. She laughed at something he said and put her hand on his shoulder. Stephanie had been trying to get him to ask her out since she had seen him back in August, but the man was either clueless or not interested. Andie suspected the latter.

She walked to the table where some of her coworkers had already staked their claim and draped her coat over the chair next to Stephanie's. Her friend soon joined her and plopped into the chair. "I swear he's never going to get the hint. I told him that I was free this weekend, but nothing. What am I going to have to do? Ask him out myself?"

"Or maybe focus on someone else."

Stephanie turned and gave her a look, one eyebrow arched higher than the other. "That tactic might work for you since you're so beautiful, but we lesser mortals don't have that option. He's the first man I've been attracted to since Peter broke up with me."

"You're an intelligent, attractive woman who has a lot to offer any man. Don't sell yourself so short." Andie didn't like it when her friends made themselves seem so much smaller than everyone else. "If that guy can't see you for the amazing woman you are, then maybe it's time to find someone who does."

Stephanie didn't seem convinced of that. Instead, she shook her head. "His name's Joe. And maybe I just need to spend more time with him. Then he'll notice me."

Andie didn't think more time would resolve the issue. She had personal experience with hoping to make something more of a relationship than what was there, and she had been left alone in the end. She rubbed at the burning in her chest. "There are more men than Joe out there who are actually interested in you."

Stephanie made a zipping motion in front of her lips as Joe joined them from the bar, carrying a mug of beer in one hand. He took a sip, then glanced at Stephanie. "Oh. I forgot to order your drink. A margarita, was it?"

She stood and glared at him. "You don't listen to any of my stories, do you? In fact, you don't hear what I'm saying at all." She turned to Andie. "You're right. I need to find a guy who appreciates who I am." Then she left the table.

Andie squelched a grin as Joe sputtered an excuse. "What's wrong with a margarita?"

"She almost died in college after drinking one because she's allergic to citrus and didn't realize it had lime juice. She's told you that story at least twice that I know of." Andie stood and shook her head at him. "You missed out on a great girl."

"Maybe not. What are you doing later?"

Seriously? She rolled her eyes and left to join her friend at the bar. "He's such a jerk. You're lucky to be rid of him."

Stephanie turned wet eyes in her direction. "I'm going to die an old maid, aren't I?"

"Oh please. If you'd actually give Dr. Henson a second look, you'd see that he's crazy about you."

Stephanie took the glass of red wine from the bartender and slid her payment across the polished wood counter. "Dr. Henson? He has a bald spot."

"He also has a kind heart and a quick smile for the children he treats for cancer." Andie gave her order to the bartender and turned to look at her friend. "You've been seeing Joe's pretty boy face rather than Dr. Henson's mature handsome features."

Her friend regarded her for a long moment. "He does wear funny ties to make those kids laugh. And you really think he's crazy about me?"

Andie raised her eyebrows at her friend. "Besides me, who in our office has bought more items from your nephew's fundraising efforts? And who brought you lunch that one time when you forgot yours at home? And who else cleans the snow off your car before you go home from work?"

"I know. You're right." Stephanie gave a nod, but it seemed to be almost hesitant. "But Dr. Henson?"

"He would remember your margarita story." Andie paid for her glass of moscato, then put her free hand on Stephanie's shoulder. "Take this weekend and think it over, but I believe you'll see what the rest of the office has noticed for months. The man is head over heels for you."

They joined the rest of their colleagues at the table.

After appetizers and a second glass of wine, Andie made her excuses and returned to her apartment. Surprisingly, she had enjoyed the evening. She usually felt out of place in a crowd as if she were looking in rather than participating in the fun. But she had been in the middle of several conversations and discovered a number of interesting facts about her coworkers. And she had surprised some of them, as well. Maybe her resolution to put herself out in the world more could pay off.

And maybe her appointment the next morning with Mr. Beckett would open up a career opportunity she'd been waiting for.

BECKETT WAITED IN the living room, glancing out the large picture window that overlooked the neighborhood. It was ten minutes before nine. Where was this woman? Cassie had assured him that her sister was a stained glass expert. If anyone could fix the window, it would be her. That is if she ever showed up. He hated being late himself, and even more the people who showed up late. In the military, early was on time and on time was late.

He hoped that she wouldn't be one of those people always running late even though she had enough time to stop for a froufrou coffee drink on her way to the house. If there was another thing he couldn't stand besides tardiness, it was sugary drinks that pretended to be coffee. Coffee was meant to be drunk hot and black. Period.

Beckett glanced around the living room of the house that he'd been working on for the last few days. After he'd won the premier Take Back the Neighborhood contest, Beckett had used his half of the quarter of a million prize money to expand his house renovation business. He had done the necessary publicity and cable television special that had been part of the prize package, but now it was time to work for himself. On himself. To prove that he could be a good person now that he was home from Iraq and hopefully erase the memories of his past there.

If only the nightmares would stop reminding him of who he really was.

A sleek silver sports car pulled into the driveway, breaking into his reverie. A brunette goddess exited the car and approached the house. No. This would not do. He didn't need any empty-headed beauty queen messing around with something that had become so important to him. He wrenched open the front door and stared at her as she stood on the porch, her hand raised to knock on the door. "You can't be the stained glass expert."

She smirked at him. "But I am."

"Why?"

The brown eyes that looked back at him seemed to glimmer with humor. "Because I did my master's thesis on the history of them in Detroit churches. And I've made a few myself. Cassie knew that I could help you out."

A master's degree? This beauty had those brains behind such deep brown eyes? "I'm confused. I didn't think she meant someone like you."

"Mr. Beckett, someone like me knows more than you about the window you found. Now, you invited me here to look at it. Since I'm here, I might as well give you an assessment."

As much as he hated to admit it, she had a point. Even if he didn't think he could hire her to fix the window, he could at least get an idea of what would be required. The idea of working side by side with such a beauty made his heart stop. She was a temptation he didn't need. He growled and shut the door behind her. "Fine. And it's just Beckett, not Mr. Beckett." He pointed to the wall. "There it is. Assess away."

She gasped and stepped forward, placing a finger on one of the broken panes. "It looks like it's most likely from the Art Deco period of the twenties. You can see how the artist used lead fillings or came to fuse the different pieces." She sighed. "Beautiful. I wonder who the artist was."

He watched her as she stared at the window, even as she backed away and removed her coat to place it over the back of a folding chair. Her eyes stayed on the window, and she approached it, putting her fingers on the glass. While she had been gorgeous getting out of her car, the light in her eyes as she looked at the window made her glow, and he was drawn to her in a way that he hadn't been to anyone since returning from war. This made him shake his head and close his eyes. He couldn't do this. Not with her. "Can you fix it?"

She ran her fingers along the cracks and answered, "No."

"I thought you were an expert."

She turned to face him, and he steeled himself from getting lost in her looks. She appeared disappointed. "Unfortunately, with a piece like this you need someone who works in repairing antiques. And I'm afraid that is out of my realm of experience." She looked over her shoulder at the window. "But it is an amazing piece."

"You've wasted my time."

She turned back to peer at him. "You asked me here to tell you what you needed to do to fix the window, not to do the repairs myself. As it so happens, I know someone who can fix it, and I'd be happy to get in contact with him."

He should have felt relief that she wouldn't be the one who would be spending time here fixing the window. Then he could say his goodbyes and not see her anymore. And yet, he regretted that she couldn't fix it. "Fine. But you can give me the number."

"No, I think this is something we need to take to him in person." She approached the window, her eyes traveling along the edges of it. "We'll need to remove the window from the wall very delicately to avoid any more damage. That I can assist you with." She ran her hands around the border of it. "Do you have a crowbar?"

"That's delicate?"

"The steel frame is wedged into the opening, but with a few careful tugs I could remove it intact." She pulled a hair tie from her pants pocket and fashioned her dark hair into a messy bun on top of her head, then she brought the ladder from the middle of the room closer to the window.

He stared at her. "Right now?"

"I thought you were eager to get this repaired."

He left the room and found a crowbar in his toolbox. When he returned to the living room, he found that Andie had climbed the ladder and was running her hands on the upper edge of the window. He handed her the crowbar and winced as she placed it between the wall and the steel frame. With light tugs, she started to loosen the window from its place. He stood below her, his hands up to catch the window if it should fall. Or the woman herself, if that was the case.

She got the upper left section free, and she gave a cry of triumph. Despite himself, he smiled at her glee at this small victory. He held up the left side of the window as she worked on the upper right corner. She started to slip back on the ladder, and he put one hand on her back to keep her upright. Just the one touch felt like heaven to him, and he had to remind himself that she was here on business. And a beauty like her had no place in his life.

Ms. Lowman continued to work at the frame with harder tugs. "This right side is more difficult to get out, and I don't want to bend the frame and damage the window more than it is."

"Shall I try?"

She stopped her work and looked at the frame once again. "No, I think if I can just get under this corner, it should come loose."

She positioned the crowbar and gave it a jerk. A crack in the window widened, and she gasped, but the entire frame came out intact from the wall. He took a hold of the left side as she kept her hands on the right and slowly descended the ladder. They took the window to a set of saw-horses he had at the other end of the living room, rested it on them, then stood back to admire it. She took her cell phone out of her pants pocket and started to take several pictures with it before lightly moving her fingers over the surface of the glass. "Who made such an extraordinary window?" She looked around the frame, but shook her head. "Whoever it was didn't sign it."

"And you really know someone who will fix it?"

She glanced up at him, and he was again struck by her simple beauty. She didn't have to use lots of makeup to enhance her looks, and he could appreciate it, if only from a distance. "He can, but I don't know if he would be willing to do so. Like I said earlier, our best bet would be to take the window directly to him for his evaluation. He works every Saturday morning at his store, but only until noon." She put on her coat and slipped her cell phone in her purse before grabbing it. "Are you coming?"

He'd hoped to spend only a few minutes with her, but it looked as if he would be spending a lot more time with this woman. And why did that idea both please and terrify him?

CHAPTER TWO

ANDIE GAVE BECKETT the directions to the glass store as she sat in the front seat of his truck, sending him furtive looks. She wasn't sure what she'd been expecting to find when she'd met him, but it hadn't been a tall, gangly man with such clear blue eyes. They had startled her at first when he'd turned them on her. Despite the flash of anger in them, she'd been intrigued. The faint scar that slashed his left eyebrow had also intrigued her.

She sent him another look, and he turned to frown at her. "Is there something on my face?"

"What? No." She quickly faced the front and motioned to the right. "We're going to turn up here at the next intersection, and then the store is positioned on the left."

"Do you always use your big words when you get nervous?"

"I'm not nervous." But her hands shook, and she clutched them in her lap to hide it. "Perhaps a slight case of nerves, but hardly worth mentioning."

He smirked at this and made the left turn into the parking lot of the glass store. "If you say so."

He shut off the engine and shifted to look at the stained glass window in the back of his truck. She had worried that it would be ruined, but he'd found old blankets that they'd wrapped it in to protect it. Hopefully, his assumption had been correct and there hadn't been any further damage.

Despite being almost six foot tall herself, she had to hop down from the truck. She joined Beckett at the back of the vehicle. He lowered the tailgate, and she held her breath as he slid the window out. "Carefully."

"Yes. I know." He practically growled the words.

They walked into the store, a bell above the door signaling their arrival. "Be right out," a voice called from the back.

Beckett laid the blanket-wrapped window on the counter and stepped away, looking at the various frames and panes of glass while they waited. Andie preferred to stay next to the glass window. Perhaps it was irrational, but she didn't want to lose sight of it. She understood the value of what Beckett had found. If Russ could restore it to its previous glory, Beckett could sell it for at least five figures. More if the artist was well-known.

A robust but old man with a few hairs fighting to stay on top of his head walked out from the back and put a hand on his chest when he spotted her. "Andromeda Lowman, what would bring you here to grace my lowly store?"

Beckett turned from the glass he'd been looking at. "Andromeda?"

She ignored the tone of his voice and started to remove the blanket. "Mr. Thorpe, I brought you something."

"We." Beckett had returned to her side. "We brought you something."

"Right. We." She gave him a nod. "We were hoping you could fix it."

The last layer of blanket pulled back, and Russ paused. "Where did you find this?"

"I'm renovating a house on Pritchard and found it behind a wall."

Russ put the glasses that rested atop his head onto the bridge of his nose and peered down at the window. "Definitely Art Deco era."

"That's what I figured." She pointed to the spokes of lead that radiated from the border's corners to the center. "These lines here confirm that assessment. As well as the color choices for the geometric border."

"Well, red and black are common choices in stained glass windows of any era." He ran a hand along the frame and said, "The artist didn't sign it."

She felt his disappointment as much as her own. "I noticed the same thing."

Beckett looked between them. "The history lesson is fine, but my question is can you fix it?"

Russ glanced up at him and returned his glasses to the top of his head. "Of course I can." They both gave a sigh of relief. "But I won't."

Andie felt her jaw drop. "Russ... Mr. Thorpe, why won't you?"

"I'm getting too old to be fixing anything. As it is, I'm in the middle of selling the business, and I'm looking forward to retirement." Russ looked down at the window and ran his fingers along the large crack on the left side. "It's too bad because this would probably be beautiful once it's restored."

She had figured that he'd be as eager to see the window restored as she was. "Is there anything we can do to change your mind?"

Beckett took a step closer to the counter. "If it's a matter of money, I can pay you whatever you want."

Russ brought his gaze up to meet Andie's, and she could almost see the gears of his brain turning. "Well, there might be something we could work out. That is, if you're willing to learn how to fix it yourself."

While the idea might thrill the artistic side of her, the practicality of the situation won out. "But this is an antique. I don't know the first thing about repairing something of this age."

"Then don't you think it's time you learned?"

She shook her head. "I don't believe that idea has any merit. My expertise is limited to more current methods of glass artistry. To gather the information and resources required would take more time than Mr. Beckett expects."

The man beside her gave a shrug. "If the window can be fixed, I have all the time in the world."

Russ gave her a smile as if he'd won. "C'mon, Andromeda. You know your fingers are itching to work with the glass. Don't you want to see the window restored to its former glory? And as he said, Mr. Beckett doesn't object to the longer time it will take."

When had it come down to her? And why was she actually considering the suggestion? "With my job, I don't have much free time except in the evenings. And I teach every other Saturday afternoon at the community center. And Sundays mean dinner with my family." The excuses seemed to roll off her tongue without any hindrance. "I don't have the hours required for this scope of a project."

"Then Mr. Beckett can learn, as well.

Between the two of you, we should be able to make it work." He turned to her cohort. "What do you say? Are you willing to get your hands dirty with fixing this window?"

Beckett turned to Andie, and she was struck by the plea in his eyes. "If you're willing, so am I. We can work out a schedule."

She looked deeper into those startling blue eyes and found herself nodding. Maybe learning how to fix the window would give her a chance to get to know this intriguing man a little better. "Fine. Yes. We can work this out."

Russ rubbed his hands together like a child anticipating the holidays. "Good. Tonight at seven, my house."

Andie paused. "Isn't that awfully quick?" Both men turned to face her.

"No better time than the present. First we have to take it apart before we can begin the repair process." Russ peered at her. "Do you have plans?"

Andie didn't want to admit that she hadn't had plans on a Saturday night for almost a year. Instead, she shook her head.

"Seven is fine." She turned to Beckett. "Will that work for you?"

He gave a quick nod. "The sooner, the better."

Well, her Saturday nights looked to be booked for the foreseeable future. And part of her couldn't wait for it to start while the other, logical part wondered what she'd gotten herself into now.

BECKETT SAT ON a stool in the basement of Mr. Thorpe's house. Built similar to the one he was renovating, he noticed. Maybe he could get some ideas for his house by seeing the layout of this one. A smile formed on his lips before he realized it, and he wondered what had gotten into him. He didn't smile. Hadn't for a long time. Trying to figure out what was going on, he felt almost hopeful. And that hadn't happened in an even longer time. Was working on the window going to give him a purpose that his therapist had been recommending he find?

Footsteps on the stairs announced another arrival. It had been little more than seven hours since he'd last seen Andie, but it was as if he'd been counting down the minutes until her appearance. The woman seemed to soothe something in his troubled mind. Part of it was her beauty, and he wondered if she could be just as beautiful on the inside. She'd already proven that she was quite intelligent and well-spoken. And given the way she'd reacted to his gruff attitude that morning, she'd shown herself to be kind and compassionate, as well.

She gave him a bright smile and walked toward him. "I was worried that I wouldn't make it in time. My art students were a little rambunctious today."

"Rambunctious?"

"Rowdy."

"I know what it means." He gazed into her deep brown eyes. "You do like your big words."

She gave him a shrug. "I like to read, so I know a myriad of big words."

Her admission made him grin. "Obviously."

Russ joined them at the worktable which was covered in what looked like a carpet remnant. With Beckett's help, they placed the window on the tabletop, and all three stepped back for a moment to gaze at it. Beckett couldn't help but again be struck by the beauty of something that was also broken and cracked. And yet its broken-ness somehow added to its magnificence. How was that possible?

Russ pointed to several stools. "Go ahead and take a seat, and we'll start your first lesson."

Beckett hadn't been in a classroom for more than a decade and had no real desire to go back. But if this would get him closer to having the window fixed, he'd sit wher-ever he was told. He chose the stool next to Andie and wondered if they should take notes.

Russ pulled out a tied leather roll and loosened it before laying it out on the edge of the table. "These are the tools that we're going to use. You're welcome to borrow mine, but I can always give you recom-mendations on where to buy your own if you choose to pursue this further."

To be honest, Beckett was here for this window, and then the knowledge would be relegated to a memory. However, Andie might be interested. She stood and leaned over the table, running her fingers along the handles of each tool. "These are exquisite. Where did you get them?"

"Most of them came from the glazier who sold me the business. They were handed down to him by his father and his father before him. Others I purchased over the years from various artists or tradespeople." Russ picked up what looked like a pencil with a roller instead of a lead point. He wedged it between his fingers with the pointer finger resting along the top of the handle. "This is my favorite glass cutter. I've tried others, but hands down it's the one I use most."

He passed it to Andie, who inspected it carefully, then returned it to him. "Mine don't look nearly as professional. I bought what was on sale."

Russ made a noise as if she got what she paid for. "If you get serious and want a future in this, then you'll need better tools."

She glanced up at him, then returned to the stool. "We'll see. I'm only committed to this window for the time being."

Russ ran a hand along the surface of the glass. "Because of the age of this window, the lead has become oxidized and brittle. That means we'll be taking the window apart and replacing the broken pieces of glass and putting it back together with new lead." He brought out a large roll of brown butcher paper. "So first we're going to make two rubbings of the original window. One will be for the design where we lay the glass pieces as we remove them. The second to be cut later as a pattern for the new glass."

Beckett and Andie both helped him place the paper over the window. Leaning over it, Russ used a piece of graphite to make rubbings of the pattern. And slowly, the design started to take shape. Seeing it reduced to paper and pencil took some of the magic away, but still, it appeared stunning.

Once both rubbings had been made, Russ put them aside, then explained how he would keep the window in a tub of water to avoid exposure to the lead and even more oxidization. Then they would use cutters to start taking apart the lead from each piece of glass. They would dry each piece of glass and match it with the appropriate spot on the pattern until the entire window had been taken apart and re-created.

Russ rubbed his hands at this point. "That's when the real work starts. Putting it back together."

Beckett felt overwhelmed already, and they hadn't even started working on the window. "How long will this take?" He knew he'd said he'd take as much time as required, but he could feel a huge chunk of his life being filled with this project. That could be good since it would keep him occupied in the evenings so that Rob wouldn't nag him to take time off from the house renovation.

Russ looked at them both, then put a hand on the window frame. "Tonight, I'd like to get the border taken off, and then we'll continue one evening next week."

Mrs. Thorpe appeared at the foot of the steps with two mugs. She handed one to Andie and the other to Russ, kissing his cheek before addressing Beckett. "Are you sure you don't want anything?"

He gave a short nod. "I'm fine. Thanks."

She patted Russ's arm before heading off upstairs. "Thanks, love," Russ told her before he shifted back to Andie and Beckett. "Now let's get down to business."

Working side by side with Andie, Beckett followed Russ's instructions on how to remove the lead from each piece of glass. He was aware of the woman beside him, a scent of lavender and something else floral wafting from the back of her neck as she bent over the tub. He stared at the nape of her neck where dark wisps of hair marked her hairline, a few strands escaping from the silver clip holding her hair in place. Russ cleared his throat and Beckett returned his eyes to the section of the border he held.

But moments later, his gaze drifted back to the elegant line of Andie's neck. When had he ever found such a sight to be so enticing? He couldn't look away. When Andie straightened with a piece of glass in her hands, he reluctantly returned his focus to his task.

After two hours, the border of the window had been removed, and the pieces of glass lay on the paper pattern. Russ took the window out of the long plastic tub and dried it with one towel before wrapping it in a second one. "Good. We'll work on the next section when we meet next Wednesday."

Once they had their tools put away for the time being, Beckett followed Andie up the stairs to the kitchen. He needed to get his mind off the woman and on to this project. He definitely didn't need her to be a distraction.

Mrs. Thorpe had set out plates and forks on the kitchen table alongside a homemade apple pie. "I hope you're hungry. It would be a shame to waste this pie."

Pie sounded good to Beckett. He couldn't remember the last time he'd had a pie made from scratch. He agreed heartily and took a seat at the table.

Stained glass windows and homemade pie. He could feel his tension lessening between his shoulder blades as he took a bite.

AFTER EATING DESSERT, Andie noticed the time. She hadn't meant to stay so late, but the pie and conversation had been more enjoyable than she'd expected. While Beckett hadn't said much, Russ was a born storyteller. Who knew the glass business was full of so many characters? She stood and sighed. "I hate to break up the party, but I need to get home. I have an early morning tomorrow."

"I'll get your coat," Beckett said as he followed Mrs. Thorpe to the living room.

Andie turned to Russ. "Thank you, Russ. I haven't had an evening like this in a long time."

"You mean boring because of us old fuddy-duddies?"

"I mean quiet, yet enjoyable." She placed a finger on her fork. "Or a pie so delicious. My mother is a fine cook, but she's not much for baking."

"I'm sure my Pattie would be more than happy to make another dessert for our next lesson." Russ turned to his wife with a look of hopeful expectation as she walked into the kitchen.

She patted his shoulder and returned his gaze. "Indeed, I would. Perhaps a strudel. Or I have a recipe for a galette that I've been meaning to try."

Russ turned back to Andie and rubbed

his hands together. "She's got that gleam in her eye. Be prepared to be spoiled."

"Oh, Russ." Mrs. Thorpe slapped the same shoulder she'd been caressing, but Andie could see the affection behind the gesture. Had her parents ever acted like this? She tried to think of a time that she'd seen them show any sign of warmth toward each other, but only recalled a faint memory of her father caressing her mother's cheek. Stronger memories of her father's absence from family activities overshadowed it.

Swallowing away the bitter thoughts, she accepted help from Beckett to put on her coat and pulled her long hair free that had gotten trapped. He gave her a nod when she thanked him. "Ms. Lowman, my pleasure."

"It's Andie. Please."

He nodded again before shrugging into his own jacket.

The Thorpes followed them to the front door. Andie turned back and smiled at them both. "Thank you again for such a lovely evening."

"We'll see you on Wednesday, then. Say about seven?"

Once all the details were agreed upon, Andie and Beckett stepped out the front door. Shivering, Andie pulled her coat tighter around herself as a frigid wind blew up the street and seemed to infiltrate the wool lining. Had the temperature dropped since they'd been inside working on the window? She glanced at her car and frowned. Not only had the temperature dropped, but snow had fallen. Almost an inch covered her car.

She started to take a step off the front porch when Beckett took a hold of her elbow. Why did his touch fluster her?

"Careful. The steps might be icy."

"I'm sure I can make it down the three steps without aid, but I appreciate the gesture."

Beckett kept his hold on her as they descended the stairs and followed the sidewalk to the driveway. Fishing her keys from her coat pocket, Andie unlocked the car doors and retrieved the snow brush from the backseat. When she straightened, she saw that Beckett had retrieved his own snow brush and was helping to clean off her car. Together, it only took a minute to remove the snow. She looked at him over the top of her car. "Thank you."

He gave her a nod. "My pleasure."

When he turned to leave, she found that she didn't want their time together to end and asked, "Would you like to go somewhere and get a drink?"

Beckett blinked at her, reminding her of an owl with big frightened eyes. "A drink? With you?"

Who did he think she meant? She gave him a smile. "Unless you're already sick of my company."

He stayed silent for a moment, then shook his head. Those big eyes shuttered quickly. "No, I don't think so."

His refusal stung a little, so Andie sighed and nodded. "Have a good night, then."

She started to get in her car when he appeared at her side. "It's not you."

"You're giving me the 'it's not you, it's me' speech? I wasn't suggesting anything more than continuing a pleasant evening." She cocked her head to the side and peered at him. "If you don't want to go, that's fine. I'll see you next week."

Beckett dropped his gaze to the ground. "I'm not into going out much, Ms. Lowman. With anyone."

"I thought you were going to start calling me Andie."

He raised his head and took a step closer to her, and her breath caught in her throat. But then he took a few steps back and gave her another nod. "I'll see you next week. Andie."

The man baffled her. Intrigued her. And she found herself looking forward to their next lesson.

CHAPTER THREE

ANDIE TOSSED THE greens with vinaigrette and then took the salad bowl to the dining room where her sister, Cassie, set down a platter with pot roast surrounded by potatoes and carrots. Her mother lit the candles while Aunt Sylvie filled the crystal goblets with water and gave a nod to them all. "Good job, girls. Dinner looks lovely."

They took their seats albeit in their new location. Last year, after her father had turned himself in to the police for embezzling from his own company, her mother sold the family home to pay back what he'd stolen and had moved in with her sister Sylvie for the time being. Sunday dinners were now held at her aunt's condo.

Conversation paused while the women passed the dishes and filled their plates with her mother's good cooking. Andie wondered how much of her adventure the day before she should share with her family. Cassie knew Beckett after all, but part of her didn't want to reveal too much too soon. It had only been one evening with the man, even if it had felt more like she'd known him for weeks.

"Andromeda, you're mooning after some man, aren't you?" her aunt asked. She turned to the other two at the table. "I know the look when a woman can't get her mind off the opposite sex."

Cassie smirked at this. "That's just Andie's usual face. She's always thinking about some man."

Hardly. Andie had thought about one man, Brian, until last year when she'd realized that nothing was going to come from it. And while she might look at men, she didn't think about them.

Until Beckett.

Her mother turned to her. "Is it anyone we know, dear?"

Andie shook her head, mortified to be drawn into the discussion like this. "There's no one." When her mother arched one eyebrow, she gave a shrug. "I thought we were going to be discussing Cassie's wedding plans over dinner."

"Nice way to change topics." Cassie put her napkin on her lap and heaved a sigh. "But yes. We do need to talk about the wedding. And more specifically, my fiancé, John. When will he be included in our Sunday dinners?"

Her mother and aunt shared looks between each other until her mother gave an imperious nod. "Once he's officially in the family, Cassandra. There is nothing wrong with spending time without him before you get married."

"And this way we can talk about him when he's not around." Andie grinned at her sister. "Now let's talk about the bachelorette party."

Her mother groaned. "You two are not going to a club to ogle men, are you?"

Cassie's head reared back as if she was offended by the idea. "Actually, I don't want a party, but I thought the Sunday before the wedding will be a special dinner with the three of us. I made a reservation at Lucido's." Cassie glanced at their aunt. "I mean four, if you'll join us, Aunt Sylvie."

The name of the restaurant brought back memories of other times the family had eaten there for special occasions. Significant birthdays. Anniversaries. High school graduations. Even celebrating her entry into the Miss Michigan beauty pageant. It had been years since the last visit. Well before her father had left. Andie realized that her sister was attempting to redeem some of their past with this dinner.

Sylvie put a hand to her chest. "I'd be honored."

Cassie shook her head. "I can't believe the wedding is a little more than a month from now. Where did the time go? It seems like John just proposed."

"And the bridal shower is this coming weekend." Their mother left the table and returned carrying a large binder stuffed with pages of notes. She turned to the appropriate section. "I confirmed the reservation at the tearoom for twenty-seven plus the bridal party. Andromeda, I have you down for arriving at noon as well as Sylvie and myself so that we can set the tables with the antique tea sets. Cassandra, you're expected at one."

"And John has to be there by four to help transport gifts. I know. We've gone over it several times." Cassie opened her own notebook by her plate. "What I want to discuss is the reception. More specifically, the father-daughter dance."

Forks poised in the air. Knives clattered to the table. Her mother choked on the sip of water she'd been drinking. "Cassandra, your father is incarcerated and will be unable to attend the wedding."

Cassie gave a nod that seemed to be tinged with regret and a little sadness. "John has a special dance with his mother, but I don't know what to do about my dance. It doesn't seem right to completely leave it out."

Andie could tell the thought of not having the dance at all made Cassie sad on a day that should be filled with happiness. "Ask Biggie or Tiny if they would step in for Daddy."

Cassie nodded slowly as she chewed. Besides being loyal employees of Cassie's, the Buttucci brothers had stepped in as honorary uncles to both of them on several occasions since they were young. "You're right. They'd both be happy to dance with me. I'll ask them. Great idea, Andie."

Another arched eyebrow from her mother. "Both of the Buttucci brothers?"

"I don't think I could decide between them, so I'll dance the first half of the song with one, then change partners." She took a deep breath. "Do you think Daddy would mind?"

Andie wanted to argue that he had lost his chance of caring whether it happened without him, when he became a thief and ruined the lives they'd known. But Cassie had always been her father's favorite, and she still seemed to care what he thought.

Truth be told, Andie too still cared about what he thought of her. If he thought of her at all.

Their mother patted her mouth with her napkin and set it down on the table beside her plate. "Your father would support whatever you wanted for the wedding. I'm sure he would approve." She gave them all a tight smile. "If you'll excuse me, I'll be back in a moment."

Their mother left the room followed closely by Aunt Sylvie. Alone with her sister, Andie turned to Cassie. "Is there ever going to be a time when the mention of Daddy doesn't send Mother out of the room to cry?"

"He was sentenced to ten years in prison. How long do you think it will take before we accept that and move on?" Cassie peered at her. "I'm planning on going to see Daddy on Saturday morning. Did you want to come with me?"

"Will we have time before the shower?"

Cassie nodded. "I haven't seen him since before Thanksgiving. I keep meaning to go visit, but other things keep popping up for this wedding, and I put it off." She reached across the table, her hand extended. "Please. It would be easier if we go together."

Seeing her father wouldn't be easy, but she agreed and put her hand in Cassie's. "I'll pick you up at eight."

Their mother and aunt returned to the dining room, and the sisters put their hands in their laps. Cassie glanced at her notebook. "There's one more thing we need to talk about for the wedding. Who is going to give me away? And before you say anything, I have an idea about that." She looked at their mother and then Andie. "I'd like you both to walk me down the aisle."

"Cassandra, I don't think—"

"Exactly, Mother. Don't think. Just hear me out." She took a deep breath. "This past year and a half hasn't been the easiest for any of us, but I always knew that I could count on you and Andie. I don't know what I would have done without you both. So will you throw convention out the window on this detail and walk side by side with me?"

Tears sprang to Andie's eyes, and she stood and walked around the table to put her arms around her sister. "I'd be honored. Thank you."

Cassie stood and hugged her back. "I know it's not the usual custom for the maid of honor to walk with the bride, but I don't care."

The two sisters, their arms around each other's waists, gazed at their mother. "What do you say, Mother?"

She rose to her feet and put her arms around them. "I don't think I could refuse such a request, do you?"

Sylvie clapped her hands as they embraced.

THE HOUSE NEEDED more work than Beckett had expected when he bought it, but he had tacked on extra weeks to the timeline. Experience had taught him that unforeseen problems popped up with regularity. This particular problem in the bathroom made him wrinkle his nose in disgust. "Black mold, you think?"

Next to him, Rob shook his head and pulled his gloves higher over his wrists. "Mold doesn't usually give off this kind of odor." He put a finger through the dark spot they'd uncovered. "This is some kind of rot. The wood framing will have to be ripped out and replaced."

Beckett had to agree. "Let's get some face masks on before we try to cut it out. In case it is black mold, it doesn't hurt to be cautious."

He left the room to retrieve the masks when he heard the whine of the saw start, then a loud clatter and a yelp. Running to help, he discovered Rob on the tile floor, the ladder on top of him. Beckett removed the ladder and crouched next to Rob. "What happened? What hurts?"

"I was going to cut out the board that held the most rot, but I leaned too far and the ladder tipped." The man winced and put a hand to his knee, trying to get off the floor.

"Don't move. You might have broken something. Let me check." Recalling his first aid instruction from his army days, Beckett held him carefully and noted his vitals since Rob had hit his head on the hard tile floor. Rob's heart rate was elevated, but his pupils seemed to be reactive, and otherwise seemed to be okay. Feeling along Rob's body, he noticed the way one leg was folded under him. Taking extreme care, he helped Rob straighten his leg. "How does that feel?"

Rob's breath came out like a hiss. "Like someone took a sledgehammer to my knee."

That's what he'd been afraid of. "If I help you up, do you think you can make it to my truck? We're going to the emergency room."

"It's just a bruise."

"It's more than that, Sergeant, and you and I both know it." He put his arms under Rob's armpits and helped the man to stand. "It's the same knee that you had replaced after Iraq, right?"

Rob grimaced as he tried to put weight on his leg. "I've felt worse."

"Nice try. We're going."

They spent the rest of the day at the emergency room while Rob got X-rays that revealed the pins in the new knee had been damaged and the implant would need to be replaced. All said, Rob faced surgery and a couple months of recuperation before he could return to work. The young man sat on the edge of the gurney staring at his feet. "I should've waited for you to come back before cutting that board."

Beckett waved off Rob's apologies. "Accidents happen."

Rob reached down to his knee and winced. "How am I going to get through a few months out of work? And you know my mom is going to insist that I move back in with her so she can take care of me."

Beckett had already planned to help the young man out where his family couldn't and insurance didn't. He was more worried about what this would do to Rob's state of mind. It hadn't been that long ago that he'd come out of a long period of depression. "Don't worry about anything. Just focus on the surgery then getting back on your feet."

Rob grimaced at his pun. "This leaves you alone to work on the house. It's going to set you back on your timeline too."

Solitude had never bothered Beckett, but a tiny part of him would miss having Rob nag him to stop working to eat lunch or go home for the day. "Maybe the quiet will be good for me."

"Or you could hire someone else."

Beckett put a hand on the man's shoulder. "I'm not replacing you, so you put that out of your head right now. You've been with me since the beginning of working on this house and the business. That counts for something."

A large woman followed by a smaller

man entered the room. She started to cry as she saw her son. "It's fine, Ma. I'll be okay." Rob seemed to enjoy her attention even as he protested.

Seeing that his friend was in better hands, Beckett excused himself. Observing families together made him remember things he'd rather forget. Like the fact that he didn't have one anymore. He'd pushed his brother away after he returned from Iraq the first time. Despite their parents being gone and that he was his only family left, he'd ignored his brother's calls and texts, hoping his sibling would get the message that Beckett wanted to be alone. Then when Simon had gotten the hint, he regretted that his younger brother had stopped bothering him. Not that he could change it. Years had passed. It was too late.

He returned to the empty work site and walked into the bathroom, staring at the rotting wood. He was better off alone.

BECKETT STOOD AT the office window of the army base's psychiatrist, and stared at the barren tree outside. It rose like black fingers trying to grasp at the gray skies above. He then turned and glanced at the clock just behind his therapist's shoulder. Shoot. Only fifteen minutes had passed since the last time he'd looked. He wanted to growl and whine, but figured that would only get him more black marks on his therapist's notepad. And he seemed to have accumulated a lot of those as the weeks had passed without any kind of breakthrough.

She followed his gaze to the clock and with a smirk on her face, said, "Talking will make the time go by quicker."

"Doubt it. Nothing to talk about."

She didn't say anything, but poised her pen above the notepad that rested on one knee. They sat for a moment in silence until he let out a huge sigh. "Fine. The nightmares have come back. Happy?"

"Why would your nightmares returning make me happy?"

"Because now we have something to talk about." He crossed his arms over his chest. "And before you ask, it's the same one. Every time. I hear Ruggirello screaming for help but I can't get to him."

She made a notation. "Have you written the letter to his widow yet?"

He gave a short nod. That had been his assignment at the last session with Dr. Samples. She had asked him to write Mrs. Ruggirello about his best friend, his comrade in arms. And he had. He'd apologized to her for not being there for her husband. For not saving him. He wished it had been him instead. Closing his eyes, he rubbed his forehead. He hadn't actually written that last part, even though it had been on his mind.

"Did you mail the letter yet?"

Rats. He should have known Dr. Samples was too smart for him. "No."

"And why not?"

"Because just writing the letter made the nightmares return. What would happen if I actually sent the blasted thing?"

The therapist sat back in her chair. "Why are you so angry?"

"I'm not."

She pointed to his crossed arms and clenched fists. "Maybe *angry* is the wrong word. Perhaps *defensive* is better."

He laughed at her words. "You use your

big words just like someone I met last weekend. She loves to trot out her vocabulary every chance she gets."

"She?"

He felt as if he'd been busted revealing something that was better left unsaid. "Don't get any ideas, Doc. She's just an acquaintance. Work related."

"And you deflected my questioning about the letter." She sat forward in her chair, resting her arms on her thighs. "When are you planning on sending it?"

Never. "Soon."

"How soon?"

He shrugged. "I don't know. There's no big rush, is there? I'll send it eventually."

"What if we put a date on that eventually? Say, before our next session?"

She wrote it down in her notes, and he wished he'd kept quiet like he'd planned. His presence at the therapy sessions might be recommended by his superiors, but that didn't mean he had to share his feelings. The less said, the better. At least that was his opinion. Switching off his feelings had kept him alive in Iraq through three tours. He became the ultimate soldier because of that fact, something the army had given him a medal for. Then they'd sent him to see a therapist when he finally came home for good.

He glanced behind her and noted that ten more minutes had passed. Rubbing his forehead, he wished that the same motion would also turn the hands on the clock.

"How are you sleeping?"

He opened his eyes to peer at Dr. Samples. "Did you miss the part where I mentioned that the nightmares are back? Every night. I try to avoid sleeping because of that."

"Lieutenant Beckett, you know that not sleeping only makes your condition worse."

He winced at the title. "It's just Beckett now. I've been discharged from the army."

"Beckett, then. You need to sleep."

She didn't understand what the nightmares did to him. His heart racing. Palms sweating. Throat sore from screaming. Body shaking. No. It was much better to avoid sleeping.

"Have you given any more thought to my suggestion of the therapy dog?"

He shook his head. The last thing he needed was to bring an animal into his life when he could barely take care of himself. He'd read the articles she'd recommended, but the benefits didn't negate the fact that he felt his entire life was a nightmare that he couldn't wake from. One he desperately wished to be free of. "I can't."

She made a note on the pad. "I'd like us to discuss this in more detail next session. And given the nightmares returning and your lack of sleep, I want to see you every week until these symptoms subside. Otherwise, you'll end up again in the ER."

He shot to his feet. "Doc, I don't need more therapy. I need…" He paused. What did he need? Could anything alleviate the despair that dogged his every step?

"That's the big question, isn't it, Beckett? What do you need?" The doctor stood and approached him, looking up into his face. "Tell me, Lieutenant."

"I told you. It's just Beckett. And I need to be left alone."

The doctor shook her head. "No, that's what you want. But if you look deep, you'll see that's not what you really need. And until you can tell me what it is you need, we'll be meeting every week. Tuesdays at four like always."

He wanted to push this tiny woman away from him. Wanted to stop the drone of voices in his head that told him that it would never get any better than this. That he was someone who didn't deserve better. But he couldn't answer the question of what he needed.

In the office building's parking lot, Beckett sat in his truck, engine running, radio blaring in order to drown out the feelings that seemed to press against his chest and were wanting to come out. He should go to the house and do more work. Without Rob being around now, Beckett made his own hours. Having free time on his hands would not help, so he put the truck in gear and started driving. Where he was driving to didn't matter as long as he was moving.

He followed traffic around downtown Detroit, taking a left at the Renaissance Center and wound up in a section of strip malls. One looked familiar, and he pulled in to find himself outside Russ's glass store. He parked close to the entrance and walked inside the shop, the bell above the door announcing his appearance. Russ called out from the back of the store, "We're closed for inventory."

Beckett started to turn and leave, but Russ walked in and spotted him. "But I could use a hand if you're free."

Beckett pointed behind him at the door. "Your front door's unlocked."

"My son must have forgotten to lock up behind him." Russ moved past him, locked the door then motioned Beckett to follow him. "Actually it was a relief to see him go. I was getting tired of his constant comments about my storage methods." He tapped his forehead. "I know where things are, and that's what matters."

Beckett followed the older man to a large room filled with sheets of glass, window frames and the detritus of a business being liquidated. He put a hand on a sheet of sky blue glass that had white swirls mixed into it. "Wow, this is amazing."

Russ turned and gave a nod. "You've got a good eye, son. That piece of glass alone is worth about a hundred bucks. Imported

German hand-rolled glass. I've got a piece of catspaw glass around here that would knock your socks off. It's a mix of purple and light amber with streaks of green." He approached Beckett. "I hate to see some of this stuff go, but what am I going to do with it in retirement?"

Beckett admired the passion in Russ's tone as he spoke about something that was mundane and everyday. "You really like glass."

"I wouldn't have spent more than forty years in the glass business if I didn't." He thrust a clipboard into Beckett's hand. "You said you'd help."

"Yes, sir."

Russ chuckled. "I knew you were military. Told my Pattie that you had to be. Afghanistan?"

"Iraq."

Russ whistled and shook his head. "Not an easy place to do a couple tours. How many did you do? I'd say at least two."

Beckett frowned. "Three. How did you figure?"

"You've got that hardened look. Like you've seen it all and would prefer to forget more." The older man looked him up and down. "I saw that look in the mirror for about a dozen years before I accepted it."

"Accepted what?"

"You can't forget. And believe me, I tried everything." Russ glanced behind Beckett. "Can you hand me that folder behind you on the worktable?"

Beckett turned and found a manila folder about four inches thick with papers. He picked it up and handed it to Russ. "You fought in World War II?"

The older man laughed until tears started to leak from the corners of his eyes, clutching the folder to his chest. "I know that I might look older than dirt to you, but that was my father's war. I saw action in Vietnam."

"How many tours?"

"Two."

The two men stared at each other for a moment until Russ nodded. "Enough of that. Let's get to work."

They worked in tandem, Russ reciting what to write on the clipboard and Beckett carefully printing it on individual lines. Their flow got interrupted by a landline phone ringing. Russ moved a stack of papers aside to answer it. "Thorpe Glass." He listened for a moment, then glanced at his watch. "Oh shoot, Pattie. Beckett and I lost track of time. We'll wrap this up, and I'll be home in ten." He glanced up at Beckett and gave a shrug. "I'll ask him. See you soon, love."

He hung up the phone. "My Pattie has invited you to join us for dinner. She's made pork schnitzel and noodles, if you're interested."

Beckett's stomach growled in response. A home-cooked dinner sounded wonderful, but his mood didn't make him good company. "Maybe another time."

"You don't know what you're missing. Pattie can cook circles around any of those celebrity chefs they show on TV." Russ took the clipboard from Beckett's hands. "I sure do appreciate your help. You saved me from about a dozen arguments with my son."

Beckett gave him a nod. "Thank you, sir."

"Thank you, son. I'll see you tomorrow night along with Miss Andromeda?"

"Yes, sir."

"Just call me Russ."

Beckett gave a short bob of his head. "Russ."

He picked up his jacket from where he'd left it and put it on, taking time to zip it up, and thrust his hands into the pockets while Russ finished turning off the lights. When they stepped outside, Beckett waited while the older man locked the inner door then pulled down an iron cage and locked that as well. Russ turned to him. "You look like you could use a good homemade meal, soldier. Are you sure you won't stop by?"

His resolve wavering, Beckett fingered the car keys in his pocket. It would be better if he got into his truck and drove home. But what was waiting for him there? Nothing but emptiness.

Sensing his uncertainty, Russ put an arm around his shoulders and steered him to his truck. "You're coming. I'm not taking no for an answer."

Beckett followed the older man's SUV to the house, wondering why he'd agreed. But then he told himself it was just dinner.

One meal. And then he could go home to his solitude.

Pattie didn't seem at all surprised to see him since she'd set a place for him at the kitchen table. He washed his hands in the small bathroom off the kitchen before taking his seat.

Conversation flowed during dinner much as it had during dessert the previous Saturday night. Beckett found himself sharing about Rob's injury. "This will put me behind on my deadline, but there's no helping it."

"You won't hire anyone else?"

Beckett shook his head. "Rob will come back once he's healed. I owe him that."

Russ gave a nod. "He was in your platoon, wasn't he?"

Had Beckett mentioned the connection? He didn't think he had. "How did you know?"

"You watch out for your men. Then and now." Russ wiped his mouth with his napkin before continuing, "You were what? Captain?"

"Lieutenant."

"And that leadership didn't end when

you came home. Even after you left the military. But you wish you could do more."

Beckett glanced around. "Am I on some kind of show with secret cameras? How do you know all this?"

Pattie reached over and took her husband's hand that rested on the table. "He thinks he can read people." She pushed the meat platter closer to him. "Help yourself to seconds, Beckett. And whatever we don't eat, I'll send home with you."

Russ pressed a kiss against his wife's hand as Beckett put more pork on to his plate. "So, about helping…"

"It sounds easier than it is, or should be. The reality is different." He lifted his knife from its place beside his plate but didn't slice into the meat. "Some don't want to be helped. And others are tired of taking orders from me. Fair enough. I had this idea of us all working together renovating houses, but it's only me and Rob."

"And by holding his job for him, you want to reward that loyalty."

"Yes, sir."

Russ paused, then broke into a broad smile. "You're a good man, Beckett. But don't be a foolish one." When Beckett started to protest, Russ held up a hand. "Listen, building a business is hard enough without doing it alone. You can't finish this house by yourself. Hire subcontractors. Temp help. And when Rob is healed, put him back to work."

Beckett knew he was right. "Thank you for the advice, sir."

Russ turned to Pattie. "I may be retired, but I still got it, don't I?" He winked at her, and she shook her head before joining in their laughter.

AFTER ANOTHER FRUITLESS job interview for the position of an elementary school art teacher, Andie decided to shake off the blues by spending time in her alma mater's library researching the stained glass window. The artist might not have signed his or her name to it, but she knew that every artist had their own unique stamp that they put on their work. She just had to figure out what that was for the window.

Andie put several search words into the computer and waited to see what came up. The artist had chosen a nautical theme.

The lighthouse. The sailboat. Even the rays of light shining from the lighthouse could be a clue to the artist's identity. Unfortunately, after about an hour of unrewarded searching, she left the library no closer to the truth than she had been when she'd started. She'd have to explore a different avenue.

Once she got home, Andie made a quick sandwich before changing out of her work clothes and into a sweatshirt and jeans. She also found a hair tie and put her hair up into a messy bun. Experience had taught her that art restoration could be untidy work. Before leaving the bathroom, she checked her makeup in the mirror, which caught her up short. What did it matter how her face looked when she had purposely dressed down? Was she really that interested in Beckett? While her head said no, her heart whispered, *Yes, please.*

Shaking her head, she turned out the light and retrieved her purse and winter coat before leaving her apartment. She drove to the Thorpe house wondering if Beckett had already arrived. His refusal to get a drink with her after their lesson last Saturday still smarted. While he said it wasn't about her, she couldn't help feeling that maybe it was. Maybe she wasn't his type. Or she was too pushy. Or…

When Mrs. Thorpe welcomed and ushered her inside, she asked, "Can I get you a mug of tea, dear? Maybe an Earl Grey this time?"

"That would be lovely. Thank you, Mrs. Thorpe."

The woman waved off the formal name. "It's Pattie. Now, give me your coat and I'll bring the tea down in a moment. Russ is waiting for you downstairs."

Andie descended the stairs to find Russ checking the pieces that they had already removed from the window. He looked up at her approach. "Andromeda, I figured it was you."

"When are you going to start calling me Andie?"

"A name like Andromeda deserves to be said and often. It's not one you hear frequently."

She shrugged. "My mother was reading a lot of Greek mythology when Cassandra and I were born."

"Ah, Cassandra, the prophetess who was never believed."

"And Andromeda is offered as a virgin sacrifice to a monster." Andie gave a shudder as she remembered the first time her mother had read that particular story to her. Why couldn't she have been named something more urbane. Alice perhaps? But then she'd have to compete with the heroine of Wonderland.

"Yes, but she was saved by a dashing hero before her demise, wasn't she?"

Andie gave a shrug. "I don't need to be saved by anybody."

"We all need saving, kiddo. Some more than others." He pointed to the tub. "I had a little time last night to work on the window, but as you can see we still have a ways to go."

Andie ran a hand along the surface of the window under water. "That's not a problem, is it?"

"I'm enjoying teaching you what it takes to restore a window. It's like my knowledge won't die with me."

"Don't talk like that." He raised an eyebrow at her tone which had come out harsher than she had intended. "I mean, you're not dying at the moment, are you?"

"We're all dying."

"When did you become so fatalistic?"

He gave a shrug. "Facing retirement will do that to you. Too much time thinking about what lies ahead of these empty years."

"Empty." She shook her head. "My guess is that Mrs. Thorpe has already planned out a road trip or two for you to take once the weather warms up. Maybe that cruise you promised to take her on?"

"She told you about that, huh?" He gave a face as if the idea was worse than death. "I just don't see how being confined on a boat is going to help me relax. I'm more likely to be calculating to see if there are enough life jackets or boats for all the passengers."

"It's not likely that you'll hit an iceberg in the Caribbean waters."

"Still, one can't be too careful. Besides, I need more than the allure of buffets and reading books by the pool to entice me."

The trudge of heavy boots on the basement stairs heralded Beckett's arrival. He handed a mug of hot tea to Andie. "Mrs. Thorpe asked me to give this to you."

She took the mug and thanked him before putting her hands around the warm ceramic to thaw them. The outdoor temperatures had turned frigid, leaving the basement cooler than their last visit.

Russ clapped his hands together. "Okay, kids. So we're going to continue taking the window apart and placing the glass pieces on our layout pattern. Any questions?"

Having none, they set to work side by side at the tub. Andie was aware of every movement that Beckett made as he cut the old lead from a piece of glass and removed the glass from the water to dry and place on the pattern. Watching his large, sturdy fingers work the knife, she found it difficult to keep her focus on the piece of glass she was supposed to detach from the window. Russ cleared his throat, and she looked up to find him smirking at her. Abashed at having been caught watching Beckett, she returned to her task.

"Do you think we'll finish taking it apart tonight?" Beckett asked.

Russ patted him on the shoulders.

"Highly unlikely, but I like your ambition, son."

Why Beckett's words gave Andie assurance was beyond her. She'd met the man less than a week ago, but already he entered her thoughts at various times of her day. She'd even dreamed of him the night before. She was hardly man hungry, but her appetite had wakened for this particular one. A part of her told her that her attraction would fade over time while another, stronger part wanted something more lasting. This part of her wanted the work on the window to take months rather than the weeks that it would require.

She removed another piece of glass and dried it off on the towel next to the pattern. One more piece of about a hundred more to go. The artist had used different sizes of glass to create the window's sense of movement in the waves and light. She pressed a fingertip to one piece and sighed.

Beckett placed a piece next to the one she had just laid. "It's a lot of time and energy, but I think it will be worth it. Don't you?"

She looked up from the glass into his piercing blue eyes. Wordless, she nodded.

He gave a shrug. "But then I guess anything worth keeping takes a lot of time and energy."

"Right."

He smiled at her, then returned to the tub. Closing her eyes, she reminded herself that she was here to work on a window. Not to get a date. Or pine after a man who wasn't interested in her.

CHAPTER FOUR

THE LINE TO get into the visiting room of the prison stretched longer than usual that Saturday morning. Andie noticed Cassie kept glancing around them and then at her watch. "We won't get very long to see Daddy if we want to make it to the shower on time," her sister said.

Andie pulled on the lapels of her coat to tug them closer for warmth. "Probably not. Should we try next week?"

"No. It has to be now. With the bridal shower today and everything else I need to do, I don't know how many more chances I'll get to come here before the wedding." Cassie checked her watch once again. "I thought they limited our visits to thirty minutes. What's taking so long?"

"Why are you so nervous? It's just Daddy." He'd torn their lives apart last year when he'd fled from the police only to turn himself in later. Her family had been paying back what he'd stolen ever since. If anyone should be nervous, it should be him to see them. Cassie skimmed her gaze over Andie before returning it to the line ahead of them. "I'm going to tell him about my dancing with the Buttucci brothers at my wedding. He's not going to like it."

"Then why tell him? It's not like he can change any of this."

Cassie eyed her before shifting back to the line. "Still trying to get on his good side, Andromeda? I thought you'd gotten over that."

"I don't have anything to get over." Even she knew that was a lie as she said the words.

Her sister guffawed, shaking her head. "Of course, you don't. You've been running after his approval for so long that you don't even recognize it anymore."

"Just because you're his favorite doesn't mean you haven't been chasing after the same just as much."

Andie tried to brush off the conversation, but her sister's words had found their mark. An ache in her chest spread as they inched farther ahead in line. Was it too much to hope that her father would one day say that he was proud of her? Even that he loved her? Cassie was right. She'd been pursuing his approval for years, but her efforts had turned out to be futile.

When they reached the head of the line and walked into the visiting room, Andie no longer wanted to see her father. Why should his approval hold her hostage? His prison sentence should have negated any hold he had on her.

And yet when he entered the room in an orange jumpsuit, her heart thudded in expectation. Maybe today he would notice her.

He approached the metal table where she and her sister sat on one side, and pulled out the chair on the other, the legs scraping on the concrete floor. Lowering himself into the seat, he gave a wince. "Are you okay, Daddy?" she asked.

Andie started to reach out, but a guard hit the table with his baton. "No touching."

Reprimanded, she returned her hands to her lap. Her father shook his head. "I'm fine. The lumpy mattress doesn't help my bad back, let me tell you. Why are you both here?" He turned to look behind them. "Is your mother here too?" Cassie shook her head, and his gaze rested on the table. "Didn't think she would be."

"Maybe if you hadn't run out on us last year."

The words were out of Andie's mouth before she could stop them. Cassie turned to her, eyebrows raised. "What Andie means is—"

"No, she's right. I hurt your mother deeply, and she hasn't forgiven me yet." Their father frowned. "I made so many mistakes. Too many. And that's on me."

This coming from the man who never apologized for anything made Andie speechless. Was all this time reflecting making a difference to him after all?

They sat quietly for a moment until Cassie broke the silence. "Today is my bridal shower. And the plans for the wedding are coming along. It's going to be a beautiful day."

"Wish I could be there to see it."

"That's what I want to talk to you about…" Cassie paused. "There are certain things that have to happen without you."

"Who's giving you away?"

Her father's gruff tone said more than his words. Cassie turned to Andie. "I've asked Mother and Andie to walk down the aisle with me."

He gave a nod, as if approving the decision.

"And I'm dancing with the Buttucci brothers for the father-daughter dance."

Her father shook his head. "No, Cass. That won't work."

"What do you mean it won't? Biggie will start, and then halfway through Tiny will cut in."

"Everyone will be thinking about me during that time. Do you really want that cloud of gloom hanging over you at your wedding?"

Cassie peered at their father. "They're already going to feel your absence. But then, like you said, that's not on me, is it?"

Daddy fell silent, his eyes lowered as if unable to face his own daughters. Andie didn't approve of what he'd done, and Cassie was right. He had gotten himself into this position. But seeing him so cowed softened her heart a tiny bit.

She longed to give him some comfort. "Daddy…" She waited until he raised his eyes to hers to continue. "Place your pillow under the part of the mattress that sags the most. That should give you some temporary comfort. And then rotate the mattress every day so that it gets equal use."

"You think you can fix my life?" He glanced around the room. "Take a look around you, Andromeda. There's no easy solution here."

Chastened, she sat back in her chair and let Cassie take the lead on the conversation. Didn't her father know that she wanted to help? Did he have to dismiss her ideas? But then he'd always done that. Even when she'd been the one behind the scenes solving the problems with deliveries or paychecks, he'd set aside her efforts as less important to his lofty home designs.

Cassie and her father talked of mostly nothing until the guard announced their half hour was over. Cassie stared at their father. "You might want to try Andie's suggestion. She's usually right about such things."

He didn't say a word but stood and followed the rest of the inmates out of the visiting room. Cassie looked at Andie. "He still thinks he knows better than us."

"Better than me, you mean." Andie crossed her arms and rubbed her shoulders at the chill in the room. "He at least listens to you."

"Not always." Cassie nudged Andie. "Let's get out of this depressing place. We've got a party to get to."

CASSIE'S FIANCÉ, JOHN, arrived near the end of the bridal shower to help with transporting the gifts. He greeted Andie with a hug and kiss on the cheek before grabbing Cassie and loving on her. It had always been her sister for John. When they'd first met, he'd barely acknowledged Andie. She'd seen that he was entirely wrapped up in her sister long before Cassie herself had.

"We appreciate your help, John," she told him when he let her sister go. "Our friends and family were quite generous."

He surveyed the table of opened gifts

and whistled. "We're going to need a bigger truck."

"Already ahead of you, son," Biggie said as he started to stack gifts in Tiny's arms.

As they went to load all the gifts into the vehicles, Andie lingered behind to make sure they didn't forget anything. As she wrapped her great-grandmother's china tea set, her mother joined her and said, "You've been quiet today."

Andie looked up from the teacup she'd been rolling in Bubble Wrap. "I guess."

"Do you want to talk about it?"

That was part of the problem. Her family didn't talk about things, but buried their hurts and disappointments deep inside. She shook her head and placed the wrapped cup into a plastic bin before starting with another.

"Cassie said you visited your father this morning."

The hurt from that morning made the burning in her chest grow warmer. Her father's rebuff had bothered her more than she wanted to admit. While it was nothing new, she should've known better. "Mother, I'm not in the mood to talk."

Her mother placed a hand on hers to still them. "You'll never be good enough for him."

Andie raised her gaze to meet her mother's. "Thank you. That's really beneficial for my gloomy mood. I feel so much better now."

She whirled around and started to gather the other tea sets that would need to be wrapped and put into the bins to transport to her mother's storage unit. Her mother followed her around the room. "I meant to say that he is the problem, not you. None of us are good enough for him. Why else would he have stolen from his own company to buy things we didn't need or want? It's all about the appearance of status to your father. And his own family didn't measure up."

"I said I would rather not discuss this." She counted the teacups and saucers to make sure they had the entire set.

"Andromeda, look at me."

She kept her eyes on the table before her, unwilling to acquiesce to the request. She didn't need to see the pain and anger in her mother's eyes to know that she'd disappointed her, as well. Instead, she closed her eyes and took a deep breath. *I'm strong. I'm capable. I'm enough.*

A cool hand on her shoulder brought her back to the moment, and she looked at her mother, who reached up and smoothed a flyaway strand of hair. "How long will you allow him to have control over your own sense of self?"

Unwilling to answer that question, Andie took a step back, and her mother dropped her hand. Andie said, "Can we just finish the cleanup? There's somewhere I need to be."

"A date?" Her mother brightened. Had it really been that long since she'd been interested in a man?

Andie didn't think she could qualify her evenings working on the stained glass window as dates. They might bring her into Beckett's presence, but as a couple they didn't relate to each other much beyond their work. She wouldn't make the mistake again of thinking that it was more than that like she had with Brian. She'd learned her lesson the hard way there. "Not tonight.

Cassie was wrong about the sparkle in my eye. There's nobody."

Her mother gave a nod and handed Andie a teacup to wrap. "Don't let your father keep you from living a full life, Andromeda. You deserve to love and be loved in return."

"Everything doesn't come back to Daddy."

"I'm glad to see you realize that."

BECKETT THRUST THE plant he'd purchased into Mrs. Thorpe's hands. "A gift for your kindness and hospitality."

She looked the plant over and nodded. "Thank you, Beckett. Russ said you had a kind soul."

Beckett didn't quite believe that. True, he had a soul, but it didn't possess an ounce of kindness. It was hard and bitter like the man he'd become. "You're welcome," he muttered and headed downstairs where Russ waited.

The older man looked up from the table when Beckett reached the bottom stair. He wore goggles and had his favorite glass cutter in his hand. Beckett approached the table and looked down at the glass that had a faint white line on it. "Want to learn how to cut glass?" Russ asked.

Beckett nodded, and the older man used what looked like pliers to break the glass at the white line. He showed Beckett how he held the glass cutter between his middle fingers before oiling the blade and applying the cutter against the pane of dark blue glass. "You want to cut edge to edge even if the piece is larger than required. You can always make smaller cuts, but always edge to edge."

The older man placed the cutter against the glass, and it made a quiet screech as he cut a triangle of glass from the larger piece. He removed the triangle and held it up for Beckett's inspection. "Want to try?"

He shook his head, feeling incompetent in the face of such skill. "What are you working on?"

"Ahh, that. Come with me." The older man stood and removed a tray from a large cabinet. "This is only part of the design. It's the biggest piece of glass art I've ever made, and I've been working on it off and on for almost thirty years."

He set the tray on the worktable to reveal

pieces of glass laid on a pattern of a bald eagle, wings spread over an American flag. The marines symbol had been drawn but not yet cut in the lower right corner.

"With retirement in my near future, I decided that I'd have more than enough time to finish this." Russ looked up at him. "What do you think?"

The design was intricate, and while Beckett might be a novice he noticed the loving care that Russ had used to bring the design to life. "Nice, but thirty years?"

Russ nodded and put the tray back into the cabinet. "Off and on, yes. Don't worry. Your window won't take nearly that long."

"Good. I don't have that much free time," Andie said behind them.

The two turned to find her rolling up her sleeves. Beckett noticed that her dark brown eyes appeared to be uncharacteristically hard and cold. "Are you okay?"

"Fine."

The word came out anything but fine, as frigid and callous as her eyes. Where was the warm, gentle woman he had met last week?

She started to work on removing the glass. Beckett glanced at Russ, who shrugged.

They made progress in silence until Russ flipped the on switch of the small transistor radio on his worktable. An oldies station played a Beatles song, and Beckett hummed along while he dried another piece of glass and placed it on the layout sheet. If they kept up this pace, they'd have all the pieces removed by next week.

"It's really coming along, isn't it?"

No one answered Beckett's question, so he returned to his spot beside Andie. Another song came on, this one a snappy Motown tune that begged to be danced to. He removed his hands from the water and dried them off on a towel before tapping Andie on the shoulder. When she turned toward him, he held out one hand. "Care for a dance?"

"We've got work to do." She turned back to the window.

Beckett tapped her shoulder once more. "It can wait. You look like you need to dance."

She looked back at him, wariness shining out of those dark eyes fringed by even darker lashes. But she put her hand in his, and he brought her body close to his. She was tall enough to meet him eye to eye, and he swallowed before starting to dance. Moving her forward and then back. Side to side. He wasn't much of a dancer, but in that basement, he felt as if he had studied the moves of Fred Astaire.

Her wariness was soon replaced with laughter when Beckett accidentally stepped on her foot. He let her go and backed away. "Sorry. I'm not that graceful."

Andie smiled at him and held out her hand. "I don't mind."

He brought her into his arms once more, and they finished the song clumsily but in a lighter mood than when they had started. Russ clapped his hands, and Andie gave a quick curtsy before returning to the tub.

Work continued without the dark cloud that had been hanging over them, and Beckett found himself again humming along to the music.

THE EVENING ENDED once again with dessert and coffee, this time a cherry strudel that had a flaky crust which melted in Andie's mouth. She closed her eyes and savored each bite, knowing that if she kept eating like this every time they worked on the window, she'd need to step up her workout regime to keep unwanted pounds off her frame.

Russ lingered over his coffee. "I think it's time for a road trip."

Andie glanced at Pattie, who watched her husband with a rapt expression. Had she finally convinced him to go on that cruise? "Where are you two heading?" Andie asked him.

"Not us. The two of you." He leaned his elbows on the table. "Some of the glass we'll need I don't carry. My pieces are more modern, but I know of a glass store up north that carries antique and specialty glass. They'd be perfect for what we need."

Beckett swallowed his bite of strudel. "How far up north?"

"Little town near Traverse City called Lake Mildred. I know the store owner and can call ahead to let Naomi know what we're looking for."

A five-hour ride in the car alone with Beckett one way? She glanced at the man, who had his fork poised halfway to his mouth. He didn't appear to be that excited about the trip. Maybe as skeptical of it as she was. "We'd have to go up on a Saturday, so I'll have to rearrange my schedule."

Russ narrowed his eyes at him. "Aren't you the boss? Can't you just decide to go up north?"

"I have contractors who depend on me for access to the site."

"On the weekends?"

Beckett seemed to have run out of excuses and returned to eating his dessert.

"I'd have to go on a Saturday I don't teach at the community center," Andie said, adding herself into the conversation. She retrieved her cell phone from her purse and pulled up her schedule. "I have a Saturday off two weeks from today. Would that suffice?"

Beckett nodded, and he returned his focus to the strudel left on his plate. "I'll rearrange things to make that work."

Russ smiled and rubbed his hands together. "Good. I'll call my friend and let her know you'll be coming to see her. This is going to be great."

Later when Beckett again walked her to her car, Andie thanked him as he held the door open for her. Before he could close the door behind her, she glanced up at him. "And thank you for the dance. I'm sorry I arrived in a surly mood, but dancing with you made it brighten."

He looked at her, and she was struck again by his piercing blue eyes. "The pleasure was mine."

"Russ seems to think we'll find what we need at this glass store."

He gave a short nod and glanced at his truck. "I don't like the idea of going so far away though."

"If this place has what we need—"

"You can see what he's doing with this road trip, right?" He turned back to her. "He's matchmaking. Russ seems to think that there's something between us and throwing us together will make something else happen."

He wasn't the only one. Pattie had cornered her to ask about the road trip with Beckett, her eyes sparkling with the idea of the two of them alone. Even part of Andie wanted to see what things could be like between them away from their regular lives for a day. Would Beckett be more accessible? Or would the unfamiliarity of their surroundings make him retreat even further?

She cleared her throat. "It's just a road trip, Beckett. Not a date."

"Exactly." He eyed her, then nodded. "Even if you are beautiful. And a woman who ought to go out."

She warmed at his compliment. "You think I'm pretty?"

He ran a hand along his jaw as if he'd said too much. "You know you are."

She thought of asking him again to join her for a drink, but the moment passed and he slammed the door shut and stalked to his own car.

BECKETT STARED AT the three dogs that sat before him. One was a golden retriever that seemed to watch him with a goofy smile. The second was a high energy Malinois that pulled at the leash the trainer had placed on him. The third looked like a black Lab, but he'd been told she was a

Labrador and German shepherd mix. She had one ear cocked forward as he watched the three dogs. Dr. Samples stepped in front of each one, telling the dog's name and different things it was capable of doing for him.

Names and abilities didn't matter to Beckett because he wasn't going to be taking any of these dogs home. He'd agreed to meet them and to consider a therapy dog, but he hadn't agreed to actually accept one. Much less start to train with it as well as house, feed and care for it.

When Dr. Samples finished talking about the third dog named Phoebe, she turned to face him, wanting an answer. He gave a shrug. "I'm still not sure that I need a dog."

"You agreed to consider it."

"And I have considered it, but I'm not convinced yet."

Dr. Samples shot him a skeptical look and waved the first dog and trainer to approach Beckett. The dog walked forward and sniffed him, then tried to jump on him. Beckett backed up. Nope, not the dog for him.

The second dog walked circles around him until the animal became distracted by noises in the hallway outside the office, straining at the leash to leave the room. The third dog sat and watched the proceedings from her spot, then lay on the floor, her head resting on her paws.

Beckett shrugged. "I don't think this is a good idea."

"No, it's a great idea. But you're not giving these dogs a chance." Dr. Samples bent down and gave the excited golden retriever a vigorous rub, cooing nonsensical words. Maybe the therapist needed a dog, but he was doing just fine.

Okay, *fine* might be too strong of a word, but he would be all right. He just needed to keep his focus on work. That's what would help him get over the nightmares and anxiety. Hard work that kept him moving without time to think. It might not be as effective a strategy as he'd hoped, at the moment, but he had confidence that it would eventually. Like it had before. "Doc, I appreciate your efforts in bringing these dogs to our session, but I doubt the right dog is here."

The words came out of his mouth, but it was as if they belonged to someone else. Heart racing, palms sweating, he tried to swallow at the bile that had risen in his throat. *Just act normal*, he repeated to himself. *This will pass. It's all okay. You're okay.*

Oblivious to his distress, Dr. Samples stood and sighed, then gave a nod to the three trainers who started to leave the office. However, the third dog glanced back at him, then jerked away from her trainer to come and stand next to Beckett. She leaned against his pant leg, and he looked down at her. Dr. Samples observed Beckett for a moment. "Are you having a panic attack?"

He took a deep breath and let it out slowly, counting to ten as she'd taught him. The dog leaned even closer to his leg, so he bent and gave her a weak pat on her head.

Dr. Samples nodded and marked something on her clipboard. "You may think that the right dog isn't here, but Phoebe obviously has other ideas."

"I don't need a dog." But he looked

down at the dark brown eyes watching him as the dog leaned closer and made a low noise in her throat. Could she really tell that he was anxious? That he felt as if the walls were closing in on him? Could a dog really sense those things?

He looked up at his therapist. "I don't know what to do with a dog."

"That's why we train you along with Phoebe so that you become a team." Dr. Samples approached the both of them. "She knew that you were having an attack and came alongside you to comfort and calm you. Did it work?"

He examined how he felt. Definitely calmer than a moment ago. His breathing and heart rate had returned to normal. He gave a slow nod. "How did she know?"

"She's been trained to recognize the signs of a panic attack." Dr. Samples leaned down and gave Phoebe a belly rub. "She'll be a good fit for you, I think."

They made plans for Beckett to meet with Phoebe again in a few days and to take her home for an overnight visit before finalizing the partnership. The trainer gave him a list of supplies he would need for the home visit. The list gave him some relief since he'd never had any pet, much less a dog. He wasn't sure what was required beyond food and water plus a place to sleep.

The trainer left the room with Phoebe, who paused to glance back at him before going.

He rubbed his face with one hand. What was he getting himself into?

CHAPTER FIVE

WITH THE WINDOW finally completely apart and the pieces laid out on the pattern, the work began on replacing the glass that had been damaged. Russ had brought several pieces from his store inventory that could be used, but Andie could see that he'd been right about needing antique glass for some of the restoration. That road trip had become a necessity.

Together, she, Russ and Beckett scrutinized each piece of glass. Those that would need to be replaced got a large X drawn in black marker. The pieces they could keep seemed to be outnumbered by two to one of those that would be replaced. Andie sighed as Russ marked another piece with the black X.

"So many."

"With some of these, you have the same glass used in different parts of the window. Replace one, you need to do them all." He marked another *X*. "Once we have all of these evaluated, we can make a list of what colors and types of glass we'll need for the project. Then we'll be on to the next step."

Beckett sighed. "So many steps…"

"That was just the beginning, son." The grin on Russ's face told her that his favorite part of the process was about to start.

Once the evaluation was complete, Russ called a time-out for a break. Mrs. Thorpe brought dessert downstairs to them on a tray that evening. Cinnamon snickerdoodle cookies had been set on a plate alongside a thermos of coffee and for Andie a mug of chamomile tea.

Andie took a cookie and her mug and sat on a stool. She'd had a job interview that afternoon before coming to the house. Thoughts of it made her sigh. Beckett took a seat on the stool next to her. "That wasn't a good sigh, was it?"

She shook her head and sipped her tea. "Didn't have a good day today."

"Want to talk about it?"

Though he had asked the question, he

didn't look as if he wanted to hear about her troubles. But if he didn't want to know, he wouldn't have asked, right? She gave a shrug. "I had an interview for a teaching position, but I don't think it went very well."

"What makes you say that?"

"They didn't say they would contact me at the end. It was just a 'thanks for your time' and then out the door moment." She broke the cookie in half and considered it. "I wasn't zealous about the job in the first place since it was part-time, but at least I'd be utilizing my degree. And it was a foot in the door, too. Which is a lot more than what I've got right now."

"I thought you taught at the community center."

"It's not a paid position at the center, and I do have bills to pay."

He gave her a look as if she'd said something ludicrous. "And that's how you evaluate a job? Whether it will pay your bills?"

It's the reason she'd gotten her degree in art education. While she might have wanted to be an artist, her mother had encouraged her to get her teaching certificate so that she'd have an alternate way to support herself. No Lowman was going to be a starving artist. "Isn't that what you're doing with construction?"

"Even if it didn't pay me a dime, I'd still work on houses." He peered at her, and she felt as if he was trying to use an X-ray machine to look into her soul. "If money was no object, what would you do?"

She took a sip of her tea to stall for time. "I don't need you to fix me."

"It's just a question."

One that she didn't want to examine too deeply this evening. They'd been enjoying themselves, and this discussion had formed a dark cloud in her thinking. "If money didn't matter, I wouldn't have taken this position."

"So maybe this wasn't the right job for you."

She had to agree with Beckett's observation. If she had been offered the teaching position, she would still need to find a second job that could coalesce with her hours in order to be able to pay her bills. It hadn't been the best fit. "You're right. It wasn't the job for me."

"Why would you want to settle then?"

"I'm not settling."

He gave her a piercing look. "What if you'd gotten the job and took it but then the perfect job came along? You're locked into a contract at this point and would have to watch as someone else got it. And all because you settled for something that was good for now, but not forever."

Wow. He was good. And he'd told her the same advice she would have given someone else in her position. "When did you get so smart?"

He gave her a smile, and she found herself smiling back at him. She bit into the cookie and felt better.

"I had an interesting day too. Looks like I'm getting a therapy dog."

The idea of the rough-and-tumble contractor with a dog amused her, and her smile deepened. "Like a service dog?"

"Phoebe would be more for emotional support rather than helping me do physical tasks." He gave an expression of chagrin. "It makes me sound so pathetic, doesn't it?"

"No." She couldn't think of the man beside her as pathetic. He had gone off to war, and she knew that the scars on returning soldiers often weren't physical. "Dogs can be wonderful."

"Do you have one?"

She shook her head. "I live in an apartment, so my life doesn't have much room for pets, much less a dog. But my sister has a big Bouvier named Evie, so I guess you could call me a dog aunt."

Beckett grinned at this. "Maybe."

She again shared his smile. "Phoebe, huh? That's an interesting name choice. In Greek mythology, Phoebe was an Amazon warrior. But that fits since you're a warrior yourself, aren't you?"

He gave a head bob and shifted in his seat, but didn't expand on his past. She wanted him to open up to her, but as soon as she'd referenced his military past, he scooted away from her. It might have only been an inch or two, but he had physically moved away from the topic. Maybe like her, he didn't want to delve too deeply into certain areas of his life. She respected his need for distance and changed the subject. "I've looked at my schedule and can go on that road trip to Lake Mildred a week from Saturday. How does that work for you?"

He gave a nod. "That should be fine. We'll need an early start that morning if we want to make this trip in one day, so I could pick you up at your apartment at seven."

Seven? Mentally, she groaned and protested, but he was right. It would be a long day, so they would need to get on the road at an early hour. She nodded. "How about I pack us a breakfast to eat on the road? And a thermos of coffee?"

"A big thermos," he answered, his smile returning. "And you've got yourself a deal."

BECKETT EYED THE dog that lay next to him on his bed. His first training session with Phoebe had gone well the other day, so now he had brought the dog home for an overnight visit. If this worked out well, the partnership would be cemented and the training would begin. But now the dog had gotten into the bed with him, and Beckett wasn't sure that he should go along with that precedent. "Off."

Phoebe blinked at him, then laid her head on her paws. Not budging. Beckett stood and pointed to the floor. "Phoebe, off."

The dog sighed, but obeyed albeit reluctantly. She took her time getting off the bed and heaved another sigh as she circled around the nest of blankets he had laid on the floor. If things worked out, he'd buy her a dog bed, but the blankets would do for the night. After several turns among the blankets and nosing them into place, she lay down and looked up at him with brown eyes that seemed to implore him to allow her on the bed.

For a moment, he almost caved in to her begging, but he shook his head. "No, you lie down there. I lie in the bed."

Phoebe let out another exasperated breath and buried her nose under her paws. Sensing he'd won this battle, Beckett positioned his pillows against the headboard and retrieved the book he'd been reading before lying down himself.

Two chapters into the story, his eyes burned with the need to sleep. He put the book on his nightstand and turned out the light, hoping for a peaceful rest.

A kid stood in the middle of the road, crying and pointing to the building next to him. Beckett pulled the truck over to avoid hitting the kid while Ruggirello got out to approach him. Beckett knew something was off. Something didn't seem right. Ruggirello handed the kid a small piece of candy, and he ran off. When Ruggirello turned to come back to the truck, a girl that looked like the kid only older threw a bomb at the truck, which exploded on impact.

Heat. Twisted metal. Trying to crawl through the open window to get to Ruggirello. But he wasn't there. Only Beckett lay on the abandoned street. He couldn't call for help. The flames and smoke choked him. He knew another explosion was coming and needed to crawl to safety. He wasn't going to make it this time. He wasn't—

Pressure on his chest woke Beckett up from the dream. He reached for his rifle before realizing he wasn't sleeping in the barracks in Iraq but his own bedroom back at home, the dog lying on his chest. He turned on the light and stared at Phoebe, who watched him with an expression of concern in her eyes. His heart rate returned to normal, and he reached over to pet the dog. She leaned up and tried to lick his chin. "I'm okay, girl. It was just a dream."

She watched him as if making sure he was really okay. He gave her a smile. "Just a dream. It's okay now."

He knew he should make her get off the bed, but waking him from the nightmare seemed to deserve a reward. He patted the space next to him. "Come on. Let's get some sleep."

After all, it was just one night.

ANDIE HADN'T BEEN able to come for the next session of working on the window, so Russ and Beckett sat on either side of the table, looking over the pieces of glass laid on the pattern. The older man picked up a fragment and held it up to the light. "See how the ripple effect makes it look like the glass is moving. You'll want to find something like this in a blue-gray or blue-green for the waves."

Beckett wrote down the information on the list they'd created for their visit to the glass store up north. "I can't convince you to come with us?" While the idea of being alone with Andie for an entire day excited him, it also scared him to death.

Russ chuckled and shook his head. "You two don't need an old fogey like me coming and interfering with your courtship."

"Courtship?"

"I know that's an old-fashioned word for a modern man like you, but it's apropos in this situation, don't you think?" Russ picked up another piece of glass and laid it back down on the pattern before peering at Beckett. "You and Andie are circling around each other like two dogs that are getting to know each other before deciding what to do."

At the word *dog*, Phoebe lifted her head from where she rested on an old overstuffed armchair in the corner of the basement. Beckett nodded to her, then turned back to Russ. "We're not circling each other."

"I've got eyes, and I see how you watch

her when she's not looking." He picked up another piece. "And how she looks at you."

Andie looked at him? Russ had to be wrong about that. Yes, he looked at Andie, but she was stunning. A man would have to be blind not to look at her. But what did he have for her to look at? He was damaged. Scarred. Maybe not where she could see it, but spending more time with him would make it clear to her very quickly. "I'm not interested in her."

"That's a lie, if I ever heard one. Son, I've been around long enough to recognize when a man wants a woman."

"I didn't say I didn't want her."

Russ raised an eyebrow at this admission. "I stand corrected."

"But nothing will come of it. I'm not looking for a relationship."

Russ gave a snicker, shaking his head. "Do you think I was looking for one when I met my Pattie? Romance was the absolute last thing on my mind, but one look and I was a goner."

"When did you two meet?"

Russ smiled and looked off in the distance. "Two months before I shipped out to Nam. I knew I wanted to marry her from the first moment I met her, but I was afraid to leave her a widow. She had other ideas, however, and she's very persuasive when she's determined. We married the week before I left."

"Just a week?"

Russ nodded slowly, still not looking at Beckett. "Her letters and the memories we made together before I left helped me get through some of the worst days of my life."

Beckett shook his head. "That didn't happen for me and my wife."

Russ seemed to shake himself from his trip to the past and glanced at Beckett's bare hand. "I didn't think you were married."

"Not anymore. Another casualty of war." Beckett ran his thumb against the base of his ring finger. He'd almost forgotten what it felt like to touch cold metal there. "She wasn't much of a letter writer. And my memories of Iraq drove a wedge between us rather than keeping us together when I came home after the second tour. I signed up for a third in the hopes of forgetting about her."

"War can do that."

Beckett turned to Russ, peering at him closely. "I don't know. You and Pattie seem to be so in love."

"Now, yes. Then?" Russ winced. "We were on the brink of divorce a couple times. She did leave me once, but she never gave up on me." He picked up another piece of glass. "This red in the lighthouse we can keep. It survived the damage."

Beckett knew the conversation had ended even if he did want to ask more. How had he turned his marriage around? How had he let go of his memories of war so that he could be in a relationship? Had he ever thought of ending it all?

Russ might have wanted to share more if Beckett had asked the right questions, but Mrs Thorpe called down that coffee was ready. The two men walked upstairs to enjoy the chocolate cake she'd made for their evening together. She had even laid aside a steak bone for Phoebe, who happily gnawed on it in the corner.

After they finished dessert and with the list of the glass they needed to replace, Beckett drove home, Phoebe lying on the passenger seat next to him. He thought about what Russ had said. And thoughts of their conversation brought others of Natalie. The last he'd heard she had married the man she'd met while he was off fighting. Well, he wished them the best. Something he could do now, but hadn't for a long time.

He parked in front of his house and looked up at its brick exterior. Memories of Natalie were strongest here where they had first lived when they got married. He'd been able to forget her most days, and eventually the nights as well once he moved to a bedroom down the hall from the one they'd shared. He whistled to Phoebe, and they walked up to the front door.

He unlocked the door and opened it to let Phoebe inside before checking the mailbox. Several envelopes indicated bills waiting to be paid, but the last one was larger and addressed in pen with a feminine hand. He checked the return address and paled. M. Ruggirello. He placed it at the bottom of the mail and walked inside the house.

He threw the mail onto the kitchen counter and checked Phoebe's food and water bowls, both needed refilling and he let the dog outside one last time before bed. Completing that, he continued his bedtime rituals of packing his meals for the next day, then retreating to his bedroom to lay out the clothes he would wear. All of his tasks finished, he had nothing left to do but go through his mail. He walked to the kitchen and opened the bills, stacking them according to the due date, then picked up the card from Ruggirello's widow. He tapped it against the counter, but couldn't find the courage to open it.

Dismissing it as something he could do in the morning, he opened the back door and whistled to the dog that looked as if she'd grown a white beard. Phoebe wagged her tail and seemed to grin up at him as he reached for a kitchen towel and wiped off the dog's jowls.

"Been eating snow, I see."

She followed him to the bedroom and lay on the large dog bed that he'd finally bought when it became clear that she was here to stay in his life. He undressed and sat on the edge of the bed. He could try to dismiss the letter that waited for him, but his mind kept going back to it. He glanced at Phoebe, who watched him with those dark brown eyes, one ear cocked high in the air. "You think I should open it, don't you?"

She looked back at him, wordlessly. He knew she wouldn't be afraid of a letter, so why was he? It wasn't the letter itself, but the words inside. Finally, he huffed and got to his feet, padding down the hall back to the kitchen. He tore open the envelope and blinked at the front of the card. "Thank You," it read.

She was thanking him? The idea of throwing it in the trash unread crossed his mind. But he'd come this far. He closed his eyes and took a deep breath before opening the card.

Thank you for your kind letter. Davey always had good words about your friendship with him. But you don't have to apologize for what happened. I hope you will always remember him as the kind friend and strong man he once was.
Marcy

He could hear his heartbeat in his ears. Putting both hands on the kitchen counter, he closed his eyes once more and tried to breathe but found that he could only take shallow gulps of air. He'd avoided Marcy at Ruggirello's funeral. Couldn't look her in the face. Couldn't say a word. He'd slipped out of the back of the church and driven in his truck as far as he could from the death of his friend. His best friend from Iraq. He'd been a coward, and that day had left him with too many regrets.

A weight pressed to his bare leg brought his attention back to the present. He looked down at Phoebe who gave a soft whine at the back of her throat. He fingered one of her silky ears. "Sorry, girl. The memories are too hard."

She looked up at him as if to agree, then she rubbed her cold nose against his leg.

Debating whether it would be safe to attempt sleep and the nightmares that would follow or to find another means of oblivion, he stood for a long time in the kitchen. Eventually, he led the dog back to the bedroom and invited her to sleep next to him. Phoebe would keep the nightmares away.

"WHAT DO YOU think of this?" Stephanie stood in front of Andie and twirled. Her coworker had changed out of her usual scrubs and into a dress. The full skirt of the dress swished around Stephanie's legs, and she wore black patent leather pumps. Definitely not a work outfit.

Andie finished powering off her computer and gave a nod. "You look really nice. Special occasion?"

The color in Stephanie's cheeks reddened. "I have a date." She peered at Andie. "With Dr. Henson."

Andie wanted to applaud. It was about time her friend gave up on Joe and focused on someone she could have a real future with. "How did that come about?"

"Well, after you suggested that he was interested in me, I started paying attention to him when our paths crossed. Trying to see what you did." Stephanie ran a hand down the front of her dress, smoothing the bodice. "And you were right, like always. He's kind and funny and maybe not the most handsome guy, but he's so sweet. And we started talking. Turns out that we have a lot more in common than I thought."

"I figured you might."

Stephanie gave a soft, wistful smile. "It's our first date tonight, and I've never been so excited about going out with a guy."

Andie hugged her friend, who jumped up and down as if she had won the grand prize. Her excitement was catching. "I'm so happy for you."

Stephanie took a step back and peered at Andie. "What are we going to do about you now?"

Andie put a hand on her chest as if to ask who she was referring to. "Who says I need to do anything?"

"Don't you think it's time you took a chance on your own life and fixed yourself?"

Fix herself? Okay, so she had wished on New Year's Eve that she could live life more fully. And she was taking steps toward that, albeit baby ones. She'd sent out more résumés this past week, and working on the stained glass window had satisfied the artistic side of herself. "I'm trying."

Using Andie's darkened computer monitor as a mirror, Stephanie applied some lipstick before looking at Andie. "What about this guy Beckett you've been talking about? And don't tell me there's nothing there. I can see the sparkle in your eyes when you bring up his name."

"We've got a project together. That's all." She might think about pursuing something more with him, but he had made it very clear that she wasn't going to get past the stone wall he'd built around himself.

"You're going on a road trip with him tomorrow, right?"

Andie shrugged. "And?"

Stephanie gazed at her with a meaningful tone. "And people can act different when they leave the familiarity of home."

"I doubt Beckett will be overcome by passion and see me in a different light."

"Stranger things have happened. Besides, you're going to be in close quarters for most of the day. You'll have a chance to get to know him a lot better." Stephanie snapped her fingers. "You said you would pack breakfast for your road trip, right? Well, they say the way to a man's heart is through his stomach. You should definitely get food that will entice him, like aphrodisiacs. Chocolate, for sure. Is coffee one of them?"

The idea of seducing Beckett with food brought a smile to Andie's lips. "Thank you for trying to be my matchmaker, but you concentrate on your own date tonight." She gave her friend a quick hug. "I have a feeling that tonight is the start of something big for you."

Stephanie returned the grin. "And tomorrow could be yours. Don't let it pass you by, Andie. You deserve happiness the same as everyone else you try to fix."

CHAPTER SIX

BEFORE BECKETT ARRIVED for their road trip, Andie double-checked the small cooler that she'd stocked with fresh fruit, sandwiches and bottles of water. She knew that she had agreed to pack breakfast for their road trip, but she figured that a light lunch wouldn't hurt either. The huge muffins she'd bought from the bakery down the street were in a separate tote bag along with small bags of chips and protein bars. The thermos held strong coffee that she assumed would please Beckett.

Her mother's oft repeated adage and Stephanie's reminder of luring a man through his stomach taunted her as she checked again. She wasn't trying to lure Beckett. Please him, perhaps. But that was as far as it went.

Her heart rate accelerated when she heard the knock on the door. Okay, so her mind said it didn't go any further, but her traitorous heart had other ideas. She opened the door and stared at the sight of Beckett wearing a navy plaid shirt, puffer vest and jeans. He seemed to fill the doorframe. She swallowed and blinked before she could speak. He looked lumberjack sexy. "Hi."

"Are you ready to go? I don't want to keep Phoebe alone in the truck for long."

He didn't seem to be as affected by her nearly as much as she was by him. She gave a nod to the cooler and tote bag. "I brought extra provisions for our trip."

"Good." He leaned over to pick up the cooler. "I guess the weatherman was wrong about the snowstorm this weekend. It hit south of the city, so the roads should be fine."

"Fortunately for us." She grabbed the tote bag, her purse and the thermos before pulling the door shut and locking it behind them. "I'd hate to put off our trip."

"Anxious to complete the window?"

She looked up at him and gave a smile. "Sure." Actually, she was more anxious about spending this time with him. To see if the rapport that they'd built while working on the window could survive away from it. "Russ gave me the directions to the store."

"And he gave me the list of what we're looking for." He patted a zipped pocket on his vest. "Shall we?"

He held his hand out so she could walk first. They walked down the one flight of stairs to the parking lot of her apartment building. A large black dog barked from the front seat of Beckett's dark red truck, and Andie stopped walking for a moment until Beckett passed her. He turned. "You're not scared of dogs, are you?"

Scared, no. But big dogs like her sister's and Beckett's made her a little nervous. "I'm not scared."

He grinned at her and opened the passenger door. The big dog jumped out and ran up to Andie. Beckett put the cooler in the truck before making introductions. "Andie, this is Phoebe. Phoebe, this is Andie and she brought us food, Phoebe, so be nice."

His words brought Andie up short. "She isn't a nice dog?"

"More like sweet and goofy." He took the tote bag from Andie as well as the thermos and stowed them behind the front seat. Whistling to the dog, he walked around to the driver's side and opened the door. Phoebe jumped in, followed by Beckett. They both looked at her through the open passenger door. "You coming?"

Reminding herself that this was a therapy dog so it wouldn't hurt her, she walked forward and got into the truck. Phoebe was wedged on the seat between her and Beckett. She fastened her seat belt and placed her purse on the floor near her feet. "Ready as I'll ever be."

Beckett chuckled as he started up the truck and drove out of her apartment complex, heading toward the highway. He turned down the volume on the radio so they could talk. "I figure we'll take a break about halfway there to stretch our legs and let Phoebe do her business. Are you okay with that?"

"Sounds good." He seemed to have everything planned, and that comforted her. She pointed to the backseat where they'd placed the food. "Are you hungry yet?"

"I'll wait until we get on the freeway."

They fell into silence as he drove, the soft strains of country music playing over the radio. It didn't seem to gel with what she knew about Beckett. "I never figured you for a country fan."

"Let me guess. A sophisticated lady like you would prefer classical music and opera."

She laughed at this. "Hardly, though my mother tried to foster an appreciation of both in my sister and me. I prefer pop music."

Beckett groaned. "Don't tell me you like boy bands?"

"What's wrong with that?" She peered around the dog to find Beckett's face screwed into distaste. "The best boy band in the world was the Beatles."

He pointed at her. "You got me there."

She chuckled as they entered the highway, and Beckett merged with the early morning traffic leaving Detroit. A few moments later, he did a hand motion for Phoebe to lie down which impressed Andie. "How did you make her do that?"

"We've been working on several hand

commands as well as verbal through our training together." He gave the dog a vigorous belly rub. "I think I'm ready for that coffee now."

She loosened her seat belt to retrieve the thermos from behind the seat as well as the travel mugs she'd packed in the tote bag. She turned around and poured him coffee in one of the mugs, then screwed the top of the thermos on tight before handing the mug over the dog to Beckett. "Black, right?"

"Thanks."

She poured her own coffee then returned the thermos to behind the seat. "I've got muffins almost the size of your head if you're interested."

"Blueberry?"

"Of course."

She grabbed the bakery bag out of the tote, and Phoebe stirred and started sniffing Andie as she pulled out a muffin and handed it to Beckett. He took a big bite then pulled off a piece and fed it to the dog. "Mmm, good. Blueberry muffins have always been my favorite."

They drove in silence again as they ate

their muffins and washed them down with coffee. The songs on the radio and the heat from the vents made the cab of the truck feel cozy. Andie unzipped her coat a little. Beckett glanced at her. "I can turn down the heat."

"No, it feels good with the blustery cold outside." She laid her head on the back of the seat, wanting to close her eyes for just a moment.

BECKETT TURNED TO glance at Andie, who had fallen asleep over an hour ago, her hand buried in Phoebe's fur. The dog had scooted closer and laid her head on Andie's lap, falling asleep, as well. The sight of them snuggled together brought a smile to his lips.

If he wanted to explore that idea further, he'd have to admit that since meeting Andie, he'd found more reasons to smile. There was something about her that made him put his guard down, to let her in just a little. If he wasn't careful, she'd burrow her way into his heart. And he couldn't let that happen.

Swallowing down the panic that thought

raised, he sat up straighter in the seat and put both hands on the steering wheel. He didn't do relationships. Hadn't his failed marriage proven that? He hadn't been able to give Natalie what she wanted, much less what she needed. She'd had to go outside of their marriage to find someone who could.

No, he was much better off alone.

The radio station started to lose its signal, so he scanned stations looking for another. Andie stirred in the seat beside him. She yawned and then stretched her arms as far as she could inside the confines of the truck. "How long have I been asleep?"

"About an hour."

She leaned her head to the left and to the right, and then reached over to pet Phoebe. "Sorry about that. I meant to stay awake and be sociable."

"It's fine." And it had been. He'd enjoyed watching her sleep with her thick eyelashes lying on her flushed cheeks. He could observe her without notice, and he preferred to keep his feelings to himself. He didn't want to think of the complications if she discovered the hold she could have on him. He cleared his throat and checked his rearview mirrors before signaling to move into the center lane. "Is it all right if we make a short stop earlier than I'd planned?"

"Sure. You're the driver." She yawned and pulled her coat around her shoulders. "Are we making good time?"

"We should get there shortly before lunchtime, so I'd say so." He checked the mirrors and changed lanes again. "I packed several blankets to wrap around the glass to transport it home."

"I didn't even think of that, so I'm glad you did. You're pretty smart."

He gave a nod, pleased at her praise. "More like practical. I've had to transport various things in my life in different weather and terrain."

"Is that what you did for the military? Transport?"

He gave a nod. "I've shipped medical supplies. Food. Troops. I got extra pay for when I had to transport explosives."

She gave a shudder. "I can't imagine the things you've seen." She reached out and put a hand on his arm. "Thank you for your service."

He winced at her words. They had never set well with him, no matter who had said them. "Don't say that."

Andie frowned. "What's wrong with it?"

He didn't answer. He'd always found it difficult to accept any thanks for what he'd done or experienced. It had been a job that he had to do, and thanks weren't necessary. And she wouldn't thank him for everything he'd done, everything he'd had to become. Unwanted memories of his time in Iraq lingered in the back of his mind, and he shook his head as if he could clear it that easily.

In silence, he took the exit to the rest area and left the truck, heading toward the bathrooms.

ANDIE WATCHED BECKETT stalk toward the men's room. What had she said that had upset him? She'd thanked him for his military service. What was wrong with that? She gave Phoebe a vigorous rub of her neck.

"Your buddy confounds me sometimes, girl. Why can't he take a compliment?"

Several minutes later, Beckett returned, but after starting the engine, they sat, idling while he stared out the windshield. After a while, he turned and looked at her, his eyes troubled yet resolute. "Please don't thank me."

His reaction still baffled her. "Why not?"

"Just don't. I don't want to talk about it, okay?"

He put the truck in reverse and pulled out of the parking spot and soon had them on the freeway. They rode with the radio as the only noise in the truck for more than twenty minutes. Finally, Andie said, "I'm sorry. I didn't know it would upset you."

"I'm not upset."

All evidence to the contrary, she wanted to say. But she let the topic drop. Instead, she brought out an orange and offered one to Beckett. He glanced at it, then back at the road. "Could you peel it for me?"

She peeled one and passed him slices between her own bites, the juice running down her chin. She searched for and found the napkins she'd packed, handing Beckett one before using one herself. "I forgot how messy these can be."

"You definitely found the juiciest orange." He stuffed the used napkin into a side pocket of his vest. "And those muffins this morning were great. I wish I could get their recipe."

"You bake?" For some reason, this surprised her. Beckett hardly looked like the type to cook his own meals, let alone pretend to be a Betty Crocker.

He nodded. "I usually bake as a stress reliever. My specialty is cakes."

This struck her as funny. "Do you decorate them with frosting? Roses and pearls too?"

"Hardly. There's nothing wrong with a simple covering of homemade frosting, especially when you beat in some cream cheese and make it thick." When she didn't say anything, he glanced at her. "What? You don't believe me?"

"I'm trying to picture you in an apron with a mixing bowl." She peered closer at him, then shook her head. "Nope. Don't see it."

"I'm a man of many talents."

She could see that she had only scratched the surface of the man Beckett was, and she longed to know more. "What's another talent you have?"

He gave it some thought, then grinned. "I can belch the entire alphabet."

This made her laugh. "Now, that I can see."

"What about you? What hidden talents do you have?"

"Well, when I competed for Miss Michigan—"

He whipped his head around and stared at her. "You did what?"

"Keep your eyes on the road, please." She shrugged and kept her gaze on the window as well. "A friend of mine told me that I could earn scholarship money by competing in beauty pageants, and she assured me that I would win. So, I did. And I won a few. I came in third for Miss Michigan. Or as my father said, second loser." She winced at the title, which still hurt eight years later.

"There were two women in the state more beautiful than you? I doubt that."

His compliment warmed her, making her smile. "Miss Michigan is more than looking pretty. It's about being talented, poised and having a platform."

"What was your platform?"

"Education for young women locally and around the world. I think it's important to invest in our teenage girls now so that they can become scientists, artists and entrepreneurs in the future." She gave another shrug as she remembered the competition. It had been fierce between her and the other four that rounded out the top five contestants. They were all beautiful and accomplished, but she'd hoped to have that something extra to put her on top. "Like I said, I came in third."

"You never said what your talent was."

"I have an ear for languages and an artistic eye which doesn't translate well to being onstage in front of an audience and a panel of judges, so I performed a modern dance routine on the advice of my pageant coach."

"They have coaches for that?"

"My father thought I could use the extra help." She remembered well the argument against getting one. She was fine as she was, but her father told her he raised her to be a winner. And winners had coaches. So she'd gotten a coach. Not that it had helped her win in the end. Something that her father repeated several times over the years. She took a deep breath, willing away how those thoughts made her feel so inadequate.

Beckett whistled, shaking his head. "Well, I say the judges were blind. You are talented and poised and beautiful. You should have won."

His words warmed her and made her heart flutter. "Thank you for that."

He stayed silent for a moment. "Ear for languages?"

"I'm fluent in French, Spanish and Italian. Plus, I know enough Arabic to ensure getting a wonderful meal and top-notch service." She gave a shrug. "Languages come easy to me."

"I struggled to get through Spanish in high school. Enough to order a taco and cerveza, at least. And ask *donde es el bano*."

She laughed at this, amused by his self-deprecating humor. "When you were in

Iraq, you didn't pick up any of the language?"

His face seemed to shutter all of a sudden, and he became quiet, sullen even. She regretted her question as she settled into the seat and ran her hand along Phoebe's short fur. She seemed to have the talent for turning off Beckett.

THE HIGHWAY STARTED to get busier the closer they reached their destination, so Beckett used that as his excuse to stay quiet and locked in his thoughts. The last couple of hours had been filled with songs from the radio rather than conversation. Which was too bad. He'd been enjoying his conversation with the former beauty queen until she'd brought up Iraq and his time there. Didn't anyone understand that he didn't want to talk about it? To dwell on it? That was the problem with his nightmares. They brought up memories that he'd rather avoid. Hoped to forget.

A sign on the side of the road advertised that they had eight miles to the exit for Lake Mildred. He pointed out the sign to Andie. "We're almost there."

She nodded, saying nothing. He shot a glance at her. "Listen. I don't like talking about my military career or the war. In fact, I don't want to talk about it at all. So please, just let it drop."

"Fine."

She might have said the word, but he could tell that it was anything but fine. It was as if he'd hurt her by shutting that part of his life off from her. But it wasn't personal. Apart from his therapist, he didn't discuss his time in the military with anyone. Not his brother. Not friends. The closest he'd come was with Russ these past few weeks. But the older man knew about war since he had lived with it too. It was easier to discuss such things with him. "I won't apologize for not wanting to talk about it."

"I didn't ask you to," she said and pulled the lapels of her coat closer around herself.

"Are you cold? I can turn up the heat."

She shook her head, so they drove on in silence. When the exit for the town arrived, he took it and turned down the radio so he could focus on the street signs as they left the freeway. "Russ said it was near the town center."

They passed several houses and reached Main Street where they saw a diner that seemed to be the center of the small town. Stores lined both sides of the street, and they passed the city hall as well as the library before finding Lake Mildred Glass Company. Beckett parked the truck and hurried around the vehicle to help Andie down. He glanced at Phoebe, who lay in the middle of the bench seat, looking at him with hopeful eyes. "Maybe we should take the dog for a walk before we go inside?"

Andie nodded as he fastened the leash to Phoebe's collar. From the glove compartment he pulled out the vest that indicated that she was a therapy dog in training and put it around the dog, who was leaning against him. He gave her a pat on her head and led her toward a snow-covered park.

Once the dog had finished her business, they walked back to the glass store. Beckett opened the door to let Andie walk ahead of them. Inside the large space, shelves lined the walls with pieces of glass of various sizes and arranged by color and style. A short woman with glasses and long graying hair pulled into a braid approached them. The name tag on her navy canvas apron read Naomi. "Can I help you both?"

Beckett pulled out the list of what they were looking for. "We were sent here by Russell Thorpe."

"Ahh, Russ. How is he doing these days?"

"Pretty well. He's retiring."

"He told me." She shook her head at the thought. "He also told me that none of his kids wanted the business. But then I'm in the same situation myself. The store will die with me, I guess." She glanced down at Phoebe who wagged her tail. "Aren't you a sweetheart?" She looked up at Beckett. "May I pet her?"

He nodded, and Naomi crouched down by the dog to give her a good scratch behind the ears. Phoebe leaned into the older woman's hand and seemed to sigh with contentment.

Once she was finished loving on Phoebe, Naomi stood and put her hands on her hips. "All right. What kind of glass are we looking for?"

"Russ gave us a list of what we need." He held out the list to her.

Naomi took it and read over it. "My modern glass is here in the front of the store, but you're looking for antique choices. Let's see what I can find you."

She led them to a separate, smaller room that had a table covered in felt at the center. Naomi checked the list again and walked to a shelf with vertical dividers. "What's the project you're working on?"

Andie pulled out her cell phone and located one of the pictures she'd taken of the window that first day they'd met. Had it really been only three weeks? Naomi gave a low whistle. "That's quite an ambitious project. Is this your first?"

"My first restoration, but I've made several smaller glass pieces," Andie answered and put her phone back into her pocket. "Russ said he'd teach us how to do it."

"He's good at teaching others as I'm sure you can tell." She consulted the list once more, then pulled out a piece of blue-green glass that looked like rippled water and laid it on the table. "This is called catspaw sheet glass." She checked a tag on it. "Made in the fifties which is later than the date of your window, but I think you could use it for the waves."

Beckett put a finger on the cool glass. It looked as if a pool of water had been poured onto the table. "Amazing. How do they do this?"

"It's a true art, isn't it?" Noise from the front room alerted them of another customer's arrival. Naomi handed the list back to Andie. "I'll let you two take a look around. If you need any help, please let me know. But take your time. I'll be back in a little bit."

She left them alone in the room, and Beckett looked over at Andie, who seemed to avoid his gaze. Any camaraderie they'd shared earlier had dissipated. He sighed and glanced around the room at the various shelves. "Where do we begin?"

Andie started to go shelf by shelf, pulling out various pieces of glass and sliding them back. "We could divide the list. Make this go a little faster."

It sounded as if she wanted to get away

from him already, and he knew he'd messed things up with her. "I don't know what we're looking for."

She held up the scrap of paper in her hand. "We have a list."

"Glass is glass to me." He gave a shrug. "I'll bow to your judgment. You're the one with the artistic eye."

She glanced at him, a half smile on her lips. "How about I pull out the glass I think will work, and we agree on them together?"

"I can live with that."

ANDIE'S BACK ACHED as she bent over the table. Straightening, she put her hands on the sore area and massaged. She wasn't sure how long she and Beckett had been in the store perusing Naomi's cache of antique glass. Time seemed to have stopped as they discussed, argued and settled on several pieces. Along with the catspaw glass for the waves, they'd agreed on a hand-rolled glass in an ombré of reds for parts of the lighthouse as well as several pieces of royal blue for the sailboat. They hadn't been able to agree on the amber glass for the light on the lighthouse, however. While several choices would have worked, none seemed to be the perfect one.

Part of her brain told her that she could make the amber glass herself. The other, saner part reminded her that she didn't do that kind of work anymore. She was a receptionist and part-time art teacher, not an artist.

But you could be again. Don't you miss it?

Shaking off the thought once more, she pulled out another piece of amber glass but dismissed it. The light from the lighthouse had to be warm and inviting. Almost as if it beckoned the sailor to safety. A place of peace.

Naomi walked into the room and nodded at the different pieces of glass they intended to purchase. "Looks like you've made some progress. If there's something you didn't find, I might be able to order it and have it shipped to you."

They took their intended purchases with them and went out into the larger portion of the store where Naomi rang up the sale. Beckett pulled out his wallet and handed the cash over. "I have blankets in my truck to protect the glass."

"I'll also wrap them in Bubble Wrap. These antique pieces tend to be more fragile than their modern counterparts."

Beckett walked out to his truck, leaving Phoebe with Andie. Naomi cut off several lengths of Bubble Wrap and swathed each piece in it before taping the edges. "You have a lot of great pieces here," Andie told her.

"What can I say? Some people collect antiques or coins. I collect glass."

Beckett returned with blankets in his arms and a concerned look on his face. His brown hair had become close to white with snow. "Andie, we've got a problem."

CHAPTER SEVEN

ANDIE LISTENED AS Beckett described the snowstorm that had come in while they'd been in the back of the store. "There's been at least four or five inches that have fallen. I don't know if there's going to be more, and I don't know what the roads going home will be like."

She walked to the door and peered out at the snow-covered truck and the white world beyond it. The snow fell at such a rate that she could barely see the outline of the building across the street. Turning to look at Beckett, she shook her head. "How long have we been here?"

He glanced at his watch. "A couple hours. But obviously long enough to make our trip home a huge question mark."

She hadn't planned on this when they'd made arrangements for this trip. What were they going to do? Where would they go? "Are you saying we're stuck here overnight?"

Naomi walked out from behind the cash register. "He's right. They're predicting another six to eight inches overnight. Salt trucks and plows won't be out until the worst of the storm is over later."

But they had nothing with them except the little food left in her cooler. The clothes on their backs. And whatever money they had in their wallets. Where would they wait out the storm? It felt a little overwhelming, and she closed her eyes for a moment. She felt a warm pressure on her leg and opened her eyes to find Phoebe leaning against her and looking up at her. "I'm okay, girl. Just a little beleaguered."

"You're trotting out the big words, so I know you're worried." Beckett approached her and put a hand on her upper arm. "We'll be fine." He turned back to Naomi. "Can you recommend a motel near here?"

"The closest motel would be in Traverse City, but we've got a bed-and-breakfast inn here that might have a vacancy." Naomi pulled out an old-fashioned rotary phone and phone book. She opened it to the page she wanted and dialed the number. "Hey, Irena. Naomi here. I've got two people in my store stranded by the snowstorm. Have you got a room?"

"Two rooms," Andie said, her cheeks reddening at the thought of being stuck in a room with Beckett overnight. "Please."

"Two rooms." Naomi listened to the person on the other end and gave a nod. "Perfect. I'll give them directions to your place. Yes, I'll be sure to tell them."

She hung up the phone. "Good news, folks. She's got a few rooms available, if you're interested."

Beckett glanced at her, and Andie turned to look outside once more. Didn't seem like they had much choice. "We're interested."

Naomi wrote the directions down on a piece of paper and handed it to Beckett. "Why don't you leave the glass here overnight and pick it up tomorrow before you leave? That way you don't have to worry about the frigid temperatures affecting the panels."

"Thank you, Naomi," he said, shaking

her hand. "We appreciate all your help. With everything."

She shook hands with Andie, as well. "You're welcome. But you might want to eat an early dinner before you go there since Irena is a fantastic hostess, but not much of a cook. She asked me to tell you to eat something before you come out to her place. Rick's diner is just down the street, it's where everyone goes."

"Thanks again, Naomi," Andie said, still feeling uncertain about the plans that were being made. She knew that traveling in the snow would be difficult, but would waiting make it better? Or would leaving while it was starting be the better choice? What if the more snow that fell put off their only chance to get home for a couple of days?

Beckett held the door open for her to walk out first. She passed by him, wondering if she should voice her concerns. They walked to his truck, and he opened the passenger door, whistling for Phoebe to jump in before helping Andie up into the truck. She turned to say something, but kept her mouth shut as he closed the door and walked to the other side of the vehicle and got inside. He put the key into the ignition, but stopped then to rub his hands. "Hungry?"

She nodded. "Yes, actually. I remember seeing the diner before we got to the store."

"Works for me."

The drive to the diner took less than a minute, and she realized they could have walked from the glass store if the sidewalks hadn't been filling quickly with deep snow. They entered the restaurant, Phoebe leaning against Beckett's leg. A woman with long curly brown hair and a clipboard in hand looked up from the cash register. "Welcome. Go ahead and sit wherever you want. We're a little light on customers with this snowstorm."

Beckett pointed at a booth near the back, taking the side that had his back to the wall but his eyes on the front door. Andie scooted down the bench opposite him and accepted the menu that the woman handed to her. "We're a full-service diner, of course, but I'd recommend my husband's burgers. They're the best in the world."

Andie gave a nod. "Sounds good."

"I'll take two. One for me, one for the dog." He reached and patted Phoebe, who lounged under the table, on her side. "No onions on hers though."

The woman wrote that on the order pad, then paused, staring at Beckett. "Maybe you get this all the time, but you remind me of someone I've seen before." She gave a shrug. "Maybe I'm just seeing things. What would you like to drink?"

Once they finished ordering their meals, Andie rested her folded hands in front of her on the table. "This overnight stay wasn't part of the trip."

"Not much we can do about the roads at this point." He nodded at the waitress, who placed a coffee in front of him and a hot tea in front of Andie. "I say we make the best of it. Is anyone waiting for you at home that you need to call?"

She considered his words. "Like my mother? I guess I should call her and let her know I might not be making Sunday dinner with the family."

Beckett sipped his coffee, seeming to hide a grin behind the mug. "I meant a boyfriend actually."

"Oh." Her cheeks burned, and she dropped her gaze to her hands on the table. "No boyfriend."

"Why not?"

She brought her gaze to his piercing blues and gave a shrug. "I broke up with someone last year, so I haven't dated in a while."

His jaw seemed to sag open a little. "Are the men around you blind?"

His attention on her made her squirm a little, so she turned the spotlight on him instead. "What about you? Is there anyone you need to call?"

"Not anymore."

"No girlfriend?"

"That either."

She gave him a smirk. "Are the women around you blind?"

He leaned in, one eyebrow arched high. "Miss Lowman, are you flirting with me?"

Yes, she was, and enjoying it more than she had with any man for a very long time. "No more than you are with me."

"I guess I am just a little." He took another sip of his coffee. "I'm afraid I'm out of practice."

"Me too."

A man came over with two plates that he placed in front of each of them. "Lizzie's bringing the dog's burger. My name is Rick. Just let me know if you need anything else."

"Rick as in this is your diner?" Andie asked.

He nodded and then smiled as his wife placed a plate in front of Phoebe. "I'm owner. Cook. And chief bottle washer."

"Unless you're making me wash them," his wife, Lizzie, muttered, but she smiled as she said the words.

Rick turned to her and returned the smile. "You love washing dishes. Admit it."

She shook her head, but kept the smile on her face as she returned to the cash register. Rick followed his wife, whispered something in her ear to which she slapped him on the shoulder and tipped her head back, laughing.

Beckett turned to Andie with a smile. "They seem to be in love."

Andie looked over at the couple and couldn't help smiling at their obvious affection for one another. "They do. They remind me of a younger version of Russ and Pattie."

He and Andie returned their attention to their meals. Andie removed the top bun off her cheeseburger to add ketchup and mustard, picking off half the onion and pickles. Replacing the top bun, she sliced the burger in half and picked up one portion. She looked up to find Beckett watching her, his own burger halfway to his mouth. "What's wrong?"

"You're fussy about what you eat."

"I don't know if *fussy* is the right word. I like it the way I like it. That's all." She took a bite, then laid the burger back on the plate next to the fries.

He gave a shrug and took a big bite of his own burger, and they continued to eat in silence. She made a pool of ketchup to dip her fries in on the side of her plate while Beckett poured lines of the stuff over his fries . She sipped her tea while he gulped his coffee.

Andie had to admit that Lizzie had been right about her husband making the best burgers. She doubted that she'd had one as juicy or flavorful in a while. And the pickles were crisp and tasted fresh. She hadn't been sure of what to expect from the diner, but the meal had been delicious. "We should come here for breakfast tomorrow before we hit the road."

Beckett nodded and accepted the tab from Lizzie. "That works for me."

He collected Phoebe, who was still licking her lips, and together the three of them walked to the register to pay. Lizzie snapped her fingers. "You were on that home renovation special in Detroit, right? You won the big prize and all."

Beckett gave a short nod. "That's me."

"I knew that you looked familiar, and it was going to bug me until I figured it out." She rang up the total on the tab. "How was everything?"

Andie noticed that they had jars of pickles for sale. She pulled out her wallet to give Beckett some cash for her portion of the bill as well as enough for one jar of the pickles, but he waved off her money. "This is my treat. You packed us breakfast and lunch after all."

She accepted his generous offer and carried the plastic bag with her pickle jar to the truck. Once inside, she stowed the jar in the cooler. She couldn't wait to share them with Cassie, who loved pickles.

Even more snow had fallen since they'd been in the restaurant, and Beckett had to clear it off before they headed for the inn. He paused and glanced behind him. "We might want to pick up some supplies we're going to need since we're spending the night. Toothpaste, deodorant and such."

He made a lot of sense, so they walked next door to the drugstore. When they entered the small store, an older man in a plaid shirt and cardigan looked up at them from where he counted money at the register. "I'm closing in five minutes. Want to get home before this snow gets worse."

Andie assured him they wouldn't be long and grabbed a small basket for their toiletries. She walked down the short aisles, choosing items she would need.

Beckett came alongside her and placed a large bag of potato chips in the basket. She looked up at him. "This is part of the necessities?"

"We're going to be trapped inside a room while it snows, so yes I need chips."

She looked at the other stuff he'd chosen. Jerky, a bag of dog treats, a few candy bars and a toothbrush. "No toothpaste?"

He gave a shrug. "I'll borrow some of yours."

The thought of them sharing toothpaste felt almost intimate. Shaking her head, she took their purchases to the front of the store. The gentleman rung them up, and Andie pulled out her wallet. Again, Beckett beat her to the punch, waving off her offer to help pay. "You can get it next time."

As they exited the drugstore, Beckett noticed a bakery that still had its lights on. "I need some cookies too."

Andie followed him into the bakery and couldn't help but smile as he eagerly looked at all the selections. The woman behind the counter introduced herself as Megs, then held a bakery box open as

Beckett chose cookies and pastries. She tied the box with a red string. "Thank you for shopping at the Sweetheart. I didn't think I'd get any more customers after the snow started, and I have a lot of inventory leftover."

Beckett added two large cups of coffee to their order. "If we hadn't been snowed in, I'm sure we would have missed enjoying your bakery."

Megs looked at him, her head cocked to one side. "Do I know you?"

"He won the home renovation contest in Detroit and appeared on a cable network special," Andie said as she added creamer and sugar to her coffee.

"That's what it is." Megs eyed him. "Do you ever do renovation work up here?"

Beckett shook his head. "I work down state in Detroit."

Megs placed a hand on her apron near where it was tied at the waist. "Too bad. My husband, Adam, and I recently found out we're expecting twins, and he came up with the perfect house for us, but it needs a lot of work."

"I'm sure you'll find someone." He paid

for their purchases and ushered Andie out of the bakery.

In the car, Andie placed their bags behind the seat and held the bakery box in her lap where Phoebe tried to get a good sniff. She watched as Beckett cleaned off the truck once again. He hadn't seemed to be comfortable with the attention he received from Lizzie or Megs. And yet he'd entered a contest that got national attention. Had it been the money that appealed to him? After all, a quarter-million dollars went a long way to alleviate any misgivings about fame. She'd have to ask him about it sometime.

Once they were on their way to the inn, Beckett drove slowly which she appreciated. She wasn't a fan of driving in snow and ice despite living in Michigan her entire life. It was a fact of life that she had learned how to steer the car when the tires wanted to go in the opposite direction. But Beckett was an expert driver, and they arrived at the inn with only minimal skidding.

The Serenity Inn was a large Victorian house with a wraparound porch. Beckett followed the circular drive that bordered the house until he found the parking section. Two other cars were parked there, so they wouldn't be the only ones at the inn. The thought both comforted and disappointed her. Not wanting to explore that reaction, she followed Beckett up the few steps to the porch. A woman in a thick Aran sweater greeted them at the front door. "Welcome to Serenity. Are you the couple Naomi sent?"

They accompanied her to an antique oak desk to register for the evening. Once they'd paid for their rooms, the innkeeper handed them their room keys which looked antique also. "I put you in adjoining rooms at the top of the stairs, if that's okay."

Adjoining rooms? Only a door away from sharing the room itself. Andie squirmed a little, but finally agreed. Since they had no luggage, they walked up the stairs to inspect their rooms. Andie turned the key in the lock and opened the door. A four-poster queen-size bed dominated the room that also contained a chifforobe and cheval mirror. A thick down comforter covered the bed that held a half-dozen pillows. It reminded her of something her mother would enjoy. She took a picture with her cell phone to show her once she returned home. Maybe her mother and aunt would like to take a road trip here someday.

Turning, she found Beckett watching her from the doorway between their rooms. "I thought I'd take a nap. Will you be okay on your own for a little while?"

She gave a nod. She'd seen a large fireplace downstairs that had a roaring fire. Sitting in front of it with a book if she could find one sounded heavenly to her. "I can entertain myself."

He gave her a short nod and retreated to his side of the door. Finding herself with time on her hands, she quickly texted her mother and sister to let them know the change of plans, then left the room to find some entertainment.

BECKETT OPENED HIS eyes and gave a start, sitting up in the large unfamiliar bed. Dusk had fallen outside, and it took a moment to remember that he was stuck in Northern Michigan with Andie during a snowstorm. He rubbed a hand over Phoebe's face, swung his legs off the bed and placed his bare feet onto the wood floor. He turned on the lamp that rested on the nightstand and pulled his socks back on. Phoebe snuffled from under the covers of the bed before crawling out to blink at him. "Want to go find Andie?" he asked her as he slid his feet into the boots he'd been wearing.

The dog wriggled out of the bed and ran to the door, waiting for him to follow her. He fastened the leash to her collar and opened the door. In the hallway, he could hear music drifting up the stairs from someone playing a piano. He followed the noise to the great room to find Andie wrapped in a blanket and seated in an armchair by the fireplace with a book. She looked up at him as he approached and smiled. Why did that sight cause his heart to stutter in his chest?

"How was your nap?"

"Good." He looked around the room to find a couple sitting at the piano, the woman playing a song as the man leaned on her shoulder. "I see you found some company."

She shut the book and scratched Phoebe

behind the ears before rising to her feet. "I did, but the loving couple is becoming a bit too much for my taste. Irena said they have board games in the dining room, if you're interested."

"All right. I'm going to take Phoebe for a short walk. And then it's game on."

Andie returned the book to a bursting bookcase. She motioned for Beckett to follow her and they walked down a hallway until it opened into a large dining room on the other side of the open fireplace. Games were gathered in a large wicker basket. After several moments of debating, they settled on a game that involved four colored sets of ten dice.

Beckett took Phoebe outdoors, but returned quickly, ruffling his hair to get the snow out of it. He took a seat at the dining table where Andie waited. "I think it's gotten worse out there. If that's even possible. I'm glad we didn't risk the drive home."

Phoebe found a spot under the table at their feet, and Beckett read the directions as Andie sorted the dice by color: red, green, blue and white. She chose the green set, so he chose blue.

Andie kept score, but it quickly became clear that she was the better player. Whether it was rolling two sets of five matching dice or one set of all ten, she would beat him twice to every one round that he won. When he only had three matching dice to her ten matching, he said, "You have to be cheating. There's no way you're that good."

She shrugged and scooped the dice into her hands, shaking them so they clinked against each other. "Beginner's luck, I guess."

He narrowed his eyes, not quite believing her. "And you swear that you've never played this game before."

She held up two fingers. "I swear."

"I think we need to find a new game so I can have a fighting chance of winning."

He walked to the basket to find another game while she stacked the dice back into their container. Finding a board game that he hadn't played since he was a kid, he pulled it out and carried it to the table. Andie groaned when he placed it in front of her. "Really? As if working on houses wasn't enough, you want to buy and sell properties too?"

He removed the lid from the box and held up a silver game piece. "I get to be the top hat."

A couple hours passed in contented amusement as they played the game until Beckett had to mortgage his last property to pay rent to Andic having landed on one of her squares. He sighed. "You're beautiful. You speak four languages fluently. And you massacre your opponents at board games. Is there anything you can't do?"

"Find a teaching job." She winced. "That sounded bitter, didn't it? It's just frustrating to have a degree that I'm not using."

"I can understand that." He tipped his top hat. "Wait here a minute. I have an idea of what we can do next."

He left the dining room and found Irena sitting in the great room with knitting needles and a ball of yellow yarn. She looked up as he walked toward her.

"Mr. Beckett, are you finding everything okay?"

"Yes, ma'am. But I was wondering if I could borrow your kitchen."

She raised her eyebrows at this request. "Planning on making something?"

"I'd like to bake a cake. I don't need a mix or anything, just basic items you'd find in a cupboard."

She seemed to consider this for a moment, then nodded slowly. "If you make a cake, I'll bring out my big coffeemaker. I'm sure we could all use some dessert on this cold snowy night. Let me know if you can't find something."

He grinned and waved. Andie was petting Phoebe in the dining room. He pulled her to her feet and held her hand, leading her toward the kitchen.

Andie glanced around the darkened room until he found the lights and turned them on. "What are we doing?" she asked.

"Irena gave me permission to bake. You want to be my helper?"

Andie nodded, so they first washed their hands at the industrial sink before Beckett started to look through cupboards. He found the ingredients he needed and searched further to find two round cake pans. After preheating the oven, he buttered the pans and set them aside. Andie had found aprons in a drawer and handed him one.

He talked her through the recipe that he knew so well he recited it off the top of his head. Together, they creamed. They sifted. They stirred. Then Beckett poured the dark chocolate batter into the waiting pans. Andie set the timer while Beckett placed the pans into the oven to bake.

While they waited for the cakes to finish baking, he showed her how to prepare a buttercream frosting from scratch with ingredients he found in the pantry. Beckett stuck his finger into the bowl then held it out tipped with frosting to Andie for her to taste. She took a step closer to him, her eyes meeting his, hesitating at first, but then licked the frosting from his finger. "Wow. That's really good."

What was good had been the way her lips parted and her tongue had darted out to taste the frosting. He tried to calm the swirl of emotions that seemed to be banging inside his chest. He wanted to taste her lips. To lick the corner of her mouth where a bit of frosting remained. Instead, he used his thumb to remove it.

Andie swallowed visibly, then licked her lips. His gaze fell to the quick dart of her pink tongue and then sank into her dark brown eyes. He started to lean toward her when the timer announced that they should check the progress of the cakes. He wanted to forget the timer, but a burnt cake wouldn't make a good impression on Andie or the generosity of the innkeeper.

He stepped back, the moment that might have happened lost as he pulled the cake pans from the oven and placed them on a set of marble trivets on the countertop. He found a toothpick and poked the center of each cake to test if it was done. It came out clean both times, so he left the cakes to cool.

When he returned his attention to Andie, she had moved to the other side of the kitchen island, rinsing their dirty dishes in the sink. Maybe the moment confused her as much as it had him. But he wasn't confused about the way he still yearned to touch her. To kiss her. It had been too long since he'd felt like this, and his heart of stone started to crumble a little at the edges.

ONCE THE CAKE was cooled, assembled and frosted, Beckett brought it out to the dining room where Irena had placed a large urn of coffee as well as a teapot with hot water for those who preferred tea. The other guests of the inn gathered in the dining room as Andie sliced pieces of cake and served them on dessert plates.

A little boy with bright red hair that stuck up in all directions licked his lips as Andie handed him a plate of cake. "Thanks, ma'am!"

"You're welcome," she answered and handed a piece of cake to the next person.

Once everyone had been served and settled into tables around the dining room, Andie passed Beckett a piece of cake before placing one for herself on a plate. While she'd served cake, he had brewed a cup of tea for her. She wondered how he knew her preference, but then they'd been working together for almost a month on the window and she'd drank many cups of tea during those sessions. It touched her that he'd remembered such a small detail.

They settled at a small table near the large picture window that looked out into the woods behind the inn. Snow still fell furiously, wind lashing it against the windows. But inside the inn, with a fire crackling in the fireplace, it felt warm and cozy.

Andie took her first bite of cake and gasped. "This is really good."

"You sound surprised."

"When you said that you were into baking cakes, I figured you used a mix, but this…" She took another bite, closing her eyes as the flavors of chocolate and a hint of cinnamon hit her tongue. "Amazing."

He smiled broadly. "Thank you for the compliment, but you helped."

As she looked into his bright blue eyes, she remembered the almost kiss between them. She'd never wanted anything more at that moment. Would have done anything to receive it from Beckett. And yet now that the moment had passed, she wondered if it would happen again. Would he ever kiss her? And why did she long for it so badly? She returned to the cake and let the rich dessert fulfill her rather than Beckett's kiss.

Once the cake was eaten and the guests returned to their activities, Andie volunteered to wash dishes, but Irena waved away the offer. "You have done enough providing this cake. Thank you."

Andie pointed to Beckett. "He's the one you should thank."

"I've never had such a moist cake that tempted me more." Irena patted Beckett on the arm as he gathered the dirty plates and forks. "You can bake for us anytime."

Beckett gave a quick nod, seemingly embarrassed by the innkeeper's praise.

After the dining room had been put back to rights, Andie yawned. The endeavors of the day had caught up with her, and the large bed upstairs seemed to call out to her. She stifled another yawn that came on the heels of the first. "I think I'm ready to turn in for the evening."

Beckett nodded. "I'll walk you to your room."

"That's not necessary. It's not that far."

"It's the gentlemanly thing to do." He

put her hand at his elbow and escorted her out of the dining room and to the stairs.

She wondered if this meant he'd try to kiss her before she retired for the evening. She wanted him to. Side by side with Phoebe between them, they walked up the grand staircase to the second floor to Andie's room. She put the key in the lock and turned to look at Beckett. The air around them seemed to spark, and she found herself powerless to turn away. Long seconds passed as they gazed at each other, but neither made a move.

Phoebe nudged Andie's leg, and she reached down to pat her. "Well, good night, then."

"Sleep tight."

She nodded and put her hand on the doorknob, but she didn't open the door. Should she make the first move? Should she press her lips against his? And yet, remembering how he'd rejected her offer for drinks on the first night they'd met, she couldn't do it. Couldn't let herself be subject to another rebuff from Beckett. Finally, she opened the door.

"Andie."

She turned at the sound of his voice. He stepped forward and swiftly kissed her cheek near the corner of her mouth. Then he walked to his own room, Phoebe trailing after him.

Andie pressed her fingers to where his kiss had landed, smiling.

CHAPTER EIGHT

ANDIE OPENED HER EYES, wondering what it was that had woken her from the sweetest dream. Silence greeted her, and she sat up in bed, straining to figure out what she'd heard.

Whimpering. Was it Phoebe? Had she been hurt? She threw the blankets off herself and strode to the door that joined her room with Beckett's and pressed her ear to hear better.

"No. No. Please don't."

Beckett seemed to be begging. She tried the doorknob, but it was locked. She turned on the light by the front door and searched to see if there was a key that would open the lock. Finding none, she returned to the door and knocked on it. "Beckett, wake up. It's me."

No answer. She tried the door again. It would swing open into Beckett's room, so maybe if she put her shoulder against it and pushed... She tried it, but it didn't open. Maybe if she pushed harder. Still locked tight.

The cries from Beckett's room grew louder, and she knew that she had to get into that room no matter what. She backed away from the door and took a run at it, slamming herself against the solid oak. Still shut. All right. One more try, and then she'd get the innkeeper for the key. She took a run at the door, slamming herself against it. It gave way, and she tumbled into the room, falling on the floor and landing on her right wrist.

She scrambled to her feet and ran to the bed where Beckett twisted in the blankets, Phoebe next to him, pawing at his arm. Andie put her left hand on his shoulder since her right hand throbbed in pain. "Beckett, wake up."

He roared at her touch and sat up in bed, backing up against the headboard, blinking but not really seeing. He seemed to be trapped in his dream world. She turned on the light beside the bed and approached him again, dropping the volume of her voice. "You're okay, Beckett. It's safe."

He blinked rapidly at her. "Andie?"

"Yes, it's me."

He looked around the room as if trying to remember where he was, then he focused on her. "I'm okay." His gaze dropped to the throbbing wrist she cradled in her hand. "But you're hurt."

"It's fine."

"How did it happen?"

She nodded toward the open door between their rooms. "I had to break down the door to get to you."

He held out his hand, and she put her right hand in his. He explored her wrist with his fingers and shook his head as she winced at the pain. "I think it's sprained, but it might be broken. We need to get you to a doctor."

"I'm fine." The last thing she needed was to try to find a doctor in the middle of a snowstorm. She'd be careful with it for a few days, and things would be fine.

"Make a fist, then."

She tried to curl her fingers in, yet the pain made her cry out loud.

"That's it. I'm taking you to the emergency room." He swung his bare legs over the side of the bed, and she found herself staring at how strong they looked, rippling with sinews yet covered in scarred skin. He glanced down to where she was looking. "You need to get dressed, and I do too."

She brought her eyes back up to meet his, then she nodded. Returning to her room, she tried to dress herself with one hand which took her a long time. Maybe Beckett was right, and she needed to see a doctor.

Once she was dressed, she walked back into Beckett's room. He hung up the phone just as he spotted her. "The nearest hospital is about ten miles away. Good thing I have snow tires and GPS to get us there. Ready?"

She nodded, amazed at how much he'd changed in just a few minutes. He'd been whimpering like a helpless child during his nightmare, and now he had taken charge of the situation. She followed him out of his room and paused as he locked the door behind them. The inn was quiet with sleeping guests, so they moved quietly down the stairs and into the foyer where Beckett turned to pull Andie's coat tighter around her. "Okay, stay here and I'll bring the truck around. The steps are likely to be icy, so be careful when you go outside."

She nodded as he handed her Phoebe's leash. He left them in the foyer and disappeared into the snowy darkness outside. Andie put her good hand on Phoebe's neck and gave the dog a reassuring massage. "It's going to be okay."

And she knew it would be with Beckett in charge. He would get them safely to the emergency room. Would get her the care she needed. Would stay by her side even as the thought of broken bones made her stomach flip. She had started the night trying to save Beckett, but it looked as if he'd turned the tables on her and was striving to help her.

Beckett pulled up in front of the inn and exited the truck to hold on to Andie's elbow as she walked down the front steps. He gave a whistle to Phoebe, who jumped into the open vehicle, then he lifted Andie in his arms to place her carefully in the truck. She turned to say something to him, but he slammed the door shut and ran around the truck to get in on the driver's side.

Once they left the inn's driveway, the voice of the GPS started to dictate their route. Beckett had turned off the radio, so the only noise in the truck besides the GPS was their breathing and Phoebe's panting. It might have made her nervous before, but knowing that Beckett was at the wheel on these icy roads gave her comfort. He wouldn't let anything happen to them.

The drive took more than a half hour on the icy roads, but Andie sighed in relief at the sight of the neon light announcing the entrance to the emergency room. Beckett pulled the truck to the entrance and was opening her door and lifting her out before she had a chance to remove her seat belt. He set her on her feet and nodded toward the automatic doors. "Go ahead and get signed in. I'll park the truck and be right there."

Then he was gone again. Despite the demons that haunted his sleep, Beckett was good in a crisis. More than good. He seemed to find a solution for every setback. She'd still be at the inn wondering if she should see a doctor if he hadn't assessed the situation and determined their course. And yet, she knew he would deny all of that. He would somehow make this all his fault rather than seeing that he was saving the day.

She went into the emergency room and checked in with the nurse at the reception desk. She looked up at Andie with a look of wariness in her eyes. "It's going to be a while, sweetie. We had a six-car pileup on the highway, so the victims have trauma priority. Sorry."

Andie nodded and cradled her hurt wrist in her hand as she found an empty chair to sit in and wait for her turn. The automatic doors of the ER opened, and Beckett strode in with Phoebe at his side, scanning faces until he found hers. He approached her and took the seat next to hers. "There's a wait because of a highway accident," she told him.

Beckett gave a short nod then stood to pick a couple of magazines off one of the empty chairs. "Here. Reading material."

She took a current events magazine and placed it on her lap, not really interested in the stories it contained. What she wanted to learn was what had made Beckett whimper in his dreams. She turned to look at him. "What were you dreaming about?"

He glanced at her, but returned his attention to the magazine. "Nothing."

"No one cries out from a dream where nothing happens."

"I didn't cry out."

She raised one eyebrow at this bald-faced lie, surprised that his pants hadn't become engulfed in flames after two lies in a row. "I know what I heard." He ignored her, keeping his nose buried in the magazine. "Fine. I'll guess what it was about."

"Please don't."

She bit her lip and gave a sigh. "I think you were dreaming about being in the Miss Michigan beauty pageant, and your batons wouldn't ignite for the talent portion."

No response. Not even a flicker of amusement or annoyance. So she figured she'd have to go even more outrageous. "Or maybe you dreamed that you had joined the circus as a clown, but your large frame wouldn't fit into the car with the other clowns. You had to stick one long leg out the window while the car zoomed around the big top."

He placed the magazine in his lap. "I know what you're trying to do, and it won't work."

"Maybe you dreamed that you were giving a speech in Congress to get more funding for research on the effects of bubble gum stuck in hair, but discovered that you were naked in front of all the senators."

"Andie..."

"You were painting a room at the house you're renovating, but didn't have any paintbrushes so you used your fingers." He shook his head. "Your toes?"

"It was nothing like that."

"So tell me." He looked at her for a long moment, and she figured he wasn't going to answer. She put a hand on his arm. "Please. We've got a long wait, and I need some conversation."

He let out a long breath and reached down to give Phoebe a reassuring pat.

Whether it was reassuring for the dog or for himself, Andie wasn't sure. "A good friend of mine died, and I was trying to save him, but I couldn't."

"In Iraq?"

He didn't look at her. Didn't nod or say a word. Seemed to be lost in his nightmare once again. He just kept patting Phoebe.

She looked at his jeans. "Is that where you got the scars on your legs?"

He blinked rapidly and said, "Yes. Our truck got hit by an IED. The front of the vehicle exploded in flames, and I was caught in the driver's seat. Couldn't get out until Ruggirello pulled me away from the truck."

"I'm sorry."

"I don't want to talk about this anymore, okay? Find something else to amuse yourself."

He stood and left the waiting room, taking Phoebe with him. He might not have shared much with her, but still she felt like she'd made some inroads with him.

He returned after a while with two paper cups of coffee, handing one to her before returning to the seat next to hers.

She thanked him and blew on the liquid before taking a sip. The brew was thick as mud and had a burnt aftertaste. She held the cup, but didn't drink any more.

Beckett smiled and finished his cup of coffee. "This is gourmet compared to some I've had."

Andie offered him her cup back. "Go ahead. I don't think I can drink it."

He took the cup from her and poured it into his own. They sat in silence, watching as other patients were called into the examination rooms. A television in the corner of the room played a movie punctuated by commercial breaks. Andie picked up the magazine. They were going to be here awhile.

A NURSE FINALLY called Andie's name. He and Andie had been waiting for more than two hours. Beckett stood and helped Andie to her feet, then trailed after her toward the nurse who looked down at Phoebe. "You can't bring the dog into the examination room."

"She's my therapy dog."

The nurse blocked his entrance. "I can

see that, but she's still not allowed back there."

Beckett looked at Andie. "I guess I'll wait for you at the chairs." He paused, noting her pale color. "Unless you need me."

She shook her head. "I'll be okay. I'll find you once they figure out what's wrong with my wrist."

Beckett gave a nod and then watched as Andie disappeared into the labyrinth of curtained rooms. He gave a whistle to the dog, who followed him back to the seat he'd abandoned a moment ago. Phoebe sat in front of him, looking at him with eyes that seemed to turn down at the corners. He reached over and scratched the top of her head. "You need a walk? Me too."

The crisp air outside kept him awake as he walked Phoebe around the grounds of the hospital. He thought of Andie getting her wrist wrapped in a cast. Probably meant she wouldn't be able to work on the window while it healed. The thought saddened him. While he didn't like how she kept trying to intrude into his personal life, he still enjoyed the time they spent together.

It wasn't the intrusion so much that annoyed him. It was because he feared what she might do if she found out the truth about him. If she knew what had happened in Iraq and forced him into retirement from the army, would she still want to be his friend? And there was always the possibility that their friendship would blur the lines into something more. Hadn't he almost kissed her earlier? He'd been so tempted to, even as he placed a kiss on her cheek, rather than on her sweet lips as he'd wanted.

Phoebe glanced back at him as if asking what he was thinking. He squatted beside the dog and petted her, resting his forehead against her. "I think that Andie could be dangerous for us."

She wasn't a dangerous person by any means, but she could cause problems for him. Especially for his bachelorhood. Since his ex-wife had left him, he hadn't thought of any woman in a romantic sense. Or any sense, if he was being honest. And here Andie was, looking at him with those big brown eyes. He wasn't sure how long he could resist her.

And resist her, he must.

Because he couldn't be in a relationship again. Hadn't tonight proven that point? The nightmares had caused her to get hurt. To break her bones. She could end up with worse if she stayed connected to him. Despite his own growing attraction for her, it would be better to end whatever this was before it became too complicated. Too involved.

Phoebe tugged on the leash, so he stood and continued to follow her around the perimeter of the hospital and returned to the warmth of the waiting room. He sat where they'd been sitting earlier so he could get a good view of Andie once she was released.

The warmth of the room made him drowsy, but he forced himself to stay awake. He couldn't and definitely wouldn't fall asleep here and risk another nightmare. Not with so many people around him. The guilt of Andie, let alone someone else, getting injured while trying to wake him still pricked at his conscience. He should make it up to her.

It was almost dawn by the time Andie came into the waiting room and searched for him. He held up his hand, then stood and gave a soft whistle to Phoebe who had been snoring from underneath his chair. He approached Andie, who held up her wrist, which was now encased in a pink cast. He wrinkled his nose. "Pink?"

She gave a shrug and ran a hand along the cast. "It's my favorite color."

He helped her put her coat on, since she struggled with the cast, then he held her elbow as they walked out of the ER. "I'll go get the car. You stay here."

"No, I want to walk."

He kept her hand on her elbow, and they trudged through the snow to where Beckett had parked the truck. He pressed the automatic button to unlock the doors and had Phoebe get in the truck cab before lifting Andie in his arms. She turned to him, those big brown eyes watching him. He could easily kiss her like this. However, he carefully placed her in the passenger seat and let the moment pass.

Once they were driving back to the inn, Andie yawned widely. "I'm so tired. And yet, I feel like eating breakfast. You?"

He glanced at her. "We could stop at

that diner again." He glanced at the clock on the dashboard. "It's after seven, so they should be open."

"I know that breakfast is part of the package deal at the inn, but I'd like to stop there, if you don't mind." She turned and looked at him, her eyes soft and heavy. "Although maybe you're tired and would rather get some sleep first."

His eyes burned with the need for sleep, but he couldn't risk that again until they returned home. "No, we'll stop for breakfast now."

"Thanks."

He nodded at her, and she settled back into the seat, her good hand scratching Phoebe's neck. The dog looked up at him as if she could get used to this. He wanted to warn her that they'd both be better off without Andie.

The diner's open sign was lit as Beckett entered Lake Mildred's Main Street, so he pulled into the slowly filling parking lot. When they entered the diner, they found a different hostess than the owner's wife who had greeted them the day before. This young girl led them to an empty table and laid two menus in front of them. Phoebe found a spot under the table and he and Andie looked through their menus. The hostess arrived with a full carafe of coffee, so Beckett turned two mugs over for her, which she filled.

Once they had ordered, Andie sighed as she glanced outside. "I don't think the snow has stopped since yesterday afternoon."

"It hasn't." He blew on his coffee and took a sip, knowing what direction the conversation was about to take. "You're thinking we're stuck here for another night."

She rested her chin on her good hand. "Don't you agree?"

"A lot can happen in a few hours. They might clear the highway by this afternoon." The thought of being stuck another night with Andie made his heart falter. He didn't know if he could do it. Distance was what he wanted. Distance before he got too attached to Andie and how she looked at him as if he was some kind of a hero. "We should be okay."

She nodded, but looked as if she hoped he was wrong.

ANDIE STARED OUT the window as the trees passed by in a blur. Beckett had been right. The roads had been cleared enough for them to return home without having to stay another night. She'd tried to delay their departure, reminding him that they both hadn't had much sleep the night before. And his had been restless because of his nightmare. Still, they'd returned to the inn and left their keys, getting on the highway after picking up the panes of glass they'd bought from the store. Those glass panels were the whole reason they'd made the road trip, but Andie felt like it had been days since they'd been in the store rather than less than twenty-four hours. So much had changed in that single day.

She glanced at her broken wrist. It still ached though the pain was tolerable without having to take any of the medication the doctor had prescribed. Broken bones aside, the tension between her and Beckett had also changed. Morphed into something akin to attraction. Affection even. She didn't want their time to end, and yet here she sat in the truck heading back to a life that didn't have him in it daily. And she really hoped she could have that once they got home.

She looked over at Beckett, who stared blearily out the windshield at the road ahead of them. He seemed as if he could use some rest. Or, at least, a pick-me-up. Noticing a sign for a coffeehouse ahead, she asked, "Could we make a quick stop? I know I could use some caffeine. And you definitely look like you could use some."

He didn't say a word, but slowed the truck and took the next exit. He pulled into the parking lot of the coffee shop. "I think I'll stay in the truck."

"You don't want to come in?"

He shook his head. "I want to go home."

Disappointment flooded her. She'd wished that he would want to keep their time together going along. To maybe explore what it was they were feeling. Obviously, she was the only one who thought the looks and almost kisses had meant more.

She opened the passenger side door and stepped down, taking her purse with her inside the coffee shop. She ordered them coffees, his black and hers with all the sugar and creams they could put in before it became something other than coffee. Thank goodness the cookies from the Sweetheart bakery were still in the backseat to give them the sugar needed to stay awake for the rest of their trip home.

When she got back to the truck, she found Beckett returning from a walk with Phoebe. He pressed the button to unlock the doors, then took the tray of coffees from her. "You didn't need to get me anything."

"I know, but I wanted to. It's my way of saying thank you for all you've done for me this weekend."

He gave a noise as if he didn't believe her. "Are you thanking me for the part where I got us stranded up north? Or how you had to break into my room to wake me up and hurt your wrist in the process?"

She stared at him, amazed that he had that kind of ego. "You're taking the blame for not only my wrist but the weather, as well?"

"It was stupid of me not to have kept an eye on the weather while we were shopping for glass."

"I could have checked as well, but the report I saw said the storm would pass south of us. We were heading north, so I thought we were safe."

He shook his head as if she didn't understand the importance of what he was saying. "I'm the driver. I should have known. Should have prepared for the possibility."

"Do you have a direct line to the weather gods for such updates? It must be nice. But we mere mortals don't."

He made a noise and glanced away from her. "Don't try to downplay what happened."

"Then don't you try to take the blame either."

He turned back to her, his ice-blue eyes warming into a hot flame of anger. "You got hurt."

She cradled the cast with her other hand. "Because of my own clumsy mistakes, not yours."

"You broke it when you were trying to help me."

"I could have gone to get a spare key, but instead I thought I was strong enough to break down the door by myself." She thought about her words. "I was pretty strong, wasn't I?"

"Don't try to belittle what happened."

"Then don't blow it out of proportion."

He stayed silent for a moment, turned and got into the truck, taking Phoebe with him on the driver's side. Well, then. Nice conversation. She opened the passenger side door and used her good hand to pull herself into the cab.

They drove for a while, but she couldn't let this go. "Your huge ego can't handle it when life doesn't go the way you planned, can it?"

"Are you psychoanalyzing me now?"

She turned in the seat to face him. "Why are you pushing me away?"

"I'm not."

All evidence to the contrary. "The closer we get to home, the quieter you get. What are you so afraid of?"

He kept his gaze out the front windshield. "Drop it, Andie."

"No. I need to know that when we get back home, you're not going to pretend that nothing changed this weekend. Because we both know it did. And that's what's scaring you. Not that I got hurt, but that you let me get close."

"Please stop."

She wanted him to understand that things like what happened this weekend weren't normal for her. She rarely got caught up in her emotions, but she'd done just that. "I think something special could happen between us, but not if you're going to shut me out before anything has started."

"Nothing can happen."

"Why not?"

"It just can't."

He looked over at her, his eyes stricken with fear and something else she couldn't identify. Grief maybe, which didn't make sense. She was still here. And she would be here for him, if he'd let her. Didn't he realize that?

The truck swerved on a patch of ice, and Beckett returned his attention to the road. Because of their safety, Andie let the conversation drop. She didn't need to upset Beckett and have them end up in a ditch.

The rest of the drive was spent in uncomfortable silence. When they finally reached her apartment complex, Beckett parked the truck and walked around to help her down, retrieved her cooler and tote bag from behind the seat. In silence, he followed her to her front door and waited as she found her key. Once inside her condo, he placed her possessions on the kitchen counter and turned to leave. "Beckett," she called after him.

He stopped in the doorway, but didn't face her. "I don't do relationships, Andie. Not anymore. And you deserve someone who does."

Then he walked out, shutting the door behind him. Andie stood in her living room, feeling as if he might as well have shut the door on any future they might have had.

CHAPTER NINE

BECKETT PULLED UP in front of the Thorpes' home and idled the engine for a moment before shutting off the truck. He'd hated to leave Andie that way. Hadn't wanted to say what he did, but she had to know that they had no future despite what she might have thought. It wouldn't be fair to her to give her false hope.

Russ met him at the front door before he had a chance to knock on it. "I was expecting you last night, son."

"We got snowed in."

The older man nodded and opened the door wider for Beckett to step inside. "I saw the weather reports and figured that's what had happened." He rubbed his hands together. "So what did you find?"

Beckett grinned at the older man's enthusiasm. "It's in the back of my truck. Care to help me bring it all in?"

"Nothing I'd like better."

Between the two men, it took two trips for them to transfer the carefully wrapped panels of glass and lay them on the worktable in the basement. Russ started to peel back the Bubble Wrap of one package and gave a whistle. "You gotta love catspaw glass. This will be perfect for the waves."

"That's what we thought."

Russ unwrapped the other pieces, commenting on each. "You have a good eye for glass."

"It was all Andie. She knows more about this kind of stuff than I do."

"Speaking of Andie, why didn't she come with you?" When Beckett didn't say anything, Russ asked, "Did something happen between you two?"

Beckett tried to find the right words, but he wasn't sure what to say or how to say it. His relationship with Andie had shifted in the couple days they'd had together. It had been like stepping into a different reality up north, but now that they'd returned home, they had to face the truth. While Beckett was attracted to her, he couldn't pursue a relationship with her.

He wouldn't. He settled on telling Russ a partial truth. "She broke her wrist, and it's in a cast."

Russ frowned as he stowed the glass on the shelves along with the pieces of the window. "How did she do that? Slip on the ice?"

If only that had been the case. "She broke the door down to my room and fell on her wrist."

"Poor girl." Russ paused, but made a face as if he didn't understand. "Why did she have to break into your room? Did you get locked out?"

"I was having a nightmare."

Russ nodded, but didn't say anything more. The two men instead discussed the plans for the week. Without Andie's help, it would be up to Beckett to work on the window under Russ's tutclage. It would slow down their progress, but it couldn't be helped. Once they agreed to meet Tuesday night, Beckett sighed. "Guess I'll be going, then."

"You have a minute? There's something else I'd like to talk to you about."

Beckett wanted to groan. Didn't anyone understand that he wasn't much for talking? That he much preferred to keep to himself. Talking didn't resolve much in his opinion. It only stirred up messy feelings. But he gave a nod. "What about?"

Russ pulled a picture from a shelf behind the worktable and handed it to him. Beckett could pick out a younger version of the man who stood next to him. "Did I tell you that I was a POW?" Russ didn't give Beckett a chance to answer, but kept talking. "By the time we were liberated, I weighed a mere ninety-five pounds." Russ placed a hand on his hefty midsection. "I know it's hard to imagine that now, but I was a bag of bones then."

"How did you survive that?"

"How did you survive what you did? You do what you have to do to get the chance to go home." Russ put a hand on Beckett's shoulder. "But just because we came home doesn't mean that what happened over there didn't follow us back."

"You had nightmares?"

Russ's serious expression relaxed. "Still do, but thankfully they are rare. The only thing that got rid of mine was time passing. I tried avoiding talking about it. Didn't work. I tried talking about it. It helped some but not enough." He shook his head. "I even tried drinking the memories away, but that failed. Even worse than anything else."

"For me, drinking usually brings up the memories." Beckett ran a hand through his short bristly hair. "Nothing helps."

Phoebe whined from the corner where she'd been resting on an old armchair and came to stand by him, staring up at him. Beckett gave a shrug. "I thought getting a therapy dog would stop the dreams, but nothing does. I keep telling my therapist that I can't keep living like this. I can't be afraid to fall asleep every night."

Russ removed his hand from Beckett's shoulder. "I understand, son, but hear me when I say that time will heal what's broken. It's not a quick fix by any means, but don't despair because it hasn't happened yet."

The thought of facing many years of feeling as he did made him understand why he'd lost more of his fellow soldiers after coming home than he had while fighting overseas. "My best friend, Ruggirello…" His voice broke, and he paused before continuing, "He killed himself because he couldn't live with the pain and the memories anymore." He cleared his throat even as his eyes burned, so he closed them. "He left a wife and two kids. And I can't stop thinking I could have stopped him. I should've known. I should've heard it in his voice." He opened his eyes and looked at Russ. "I should have stopped him."

"Did he tell you that he was thinking of suicide?"

Beckett shook his head. He'd gone over his last conversation with Ruggirello, trying to find clues of what his friend had been thinking. But not knowing didn't exonerate him from fault. "I was his best friend. How could I have not known?"

"Was he able to read your mind? Did he know what you were thinking every minute of every day?"

That was ridiculous. No one knew what Beckett was thinking all the time. Most of the time, he didn't know himself. "No, he couldn't know." Russ didn't say a word but held his hands palms up. Beckett shook his head. "That's not a good enough answer. He's dead, and I didn't see it coming. I should have."

"Why you? Why not his wife? His doctor?"

He couldn't accept that. Buddies told each other everything. Ruggirello could have told him that his situation was getting desperate. He could have told him, and Beckett would have found a way to help his friend. But he had to live every day with the knowledge that he had done nothing. "You just don't get it, Russ."

"So explain it to me."

Russ couldn't understand. Not that Beckett did, but he had a better insight into his relationship with Ruggirello. "I can't."

"Sure you can. Just tell me what keeps your nightmares coming back." Russ took a step closer to Beckett. "What do you dream about?"

Beckett shook his head even more. He couldn't say it. Wouldn't say it. Russ took another step toward him. "What do you see before you wake up?"

"He saved my life, but I couldn't save his!"

The words hung in the air. Beckett had said them aloud, and there was no way to take them back now. But he wasn't sure he wanted to. Saying them had released the tightness in his chest. Had loosened the vise that squeezed his neck. He took a deep breath. "Why couldn't I save him?"

Beckett crouched, dropping to his knees and burying his face into Phoebe's fur. Russ put his hand on his shoulder. "Unfortunately, we can't save everyone. Some don't want to be."

Had Ruggirello given up to the point where he hadn't wanted to be saved? Is that why he hadn't said a word? "He had so much to live for."

"And so do you, son. Don't you forget that." Russ paused again. "I know you don't like talking, but there's a group of us veterans that meet once a month at someone's house. We take turns hosting, and my turn is in a couple of weeks. Would you like to join us?"

More talking about things he couldn't change? Or hearing memories of war that others shared? "I don't think that's a good idea."

"Because you're assuming we'll make you talk about what happened over there? First of all, no one talks that doesn't want to. Period. Second of all, we don't discuss what happened during our service. Most of the time, we just eat and talk about nothing important. It actually helps."

Beckett looked up at Russ. "I don't do well with groups of people."

"Just think about it. That's all I'm asking."

CASSIE STOPPED BY Andie's apartment, bringing John with her as well as a caramel apple pie that John's mother had baked. "You missed Sunday dinner, but there's no reason to miss out on dessert," Cassie said as she breezed through the door.

Andie retrieved plates from her cupboard and found a knife to cut the pie into thick wedges. She served it with mugs of coffee at her dining room table before taking a seat herself. "So what did I miss?"

Cassie shrugged. "John's still not included at family dinners until after the wedding." She took a large bite of pie and moaned. "Oh, babe. Your mom bakes an amazing pie."

He wiggled his eyebrows. "It's one of the reasons you're marrying me."

"Got that right." She took another bite and swallowed before continuing on what Andie had missed. "We finalized the plans for the reception. You are coming to help decorate the night before, right?"

As if Andie wouldn't follow through with her promise. "Aren't I your maid of honor? Although this wrist might slow me down some."

"Well, I need to nail down some of these commitments."

"And my mom is hosting the rehearsal dinner at her house after we decorate." John gave a wry grin. "The wedding is still two weeks away, but you'd think it was this weekend the way she is frantically cleaning. And giving me more to-do lists."

"How are she and Biggie getting along?"

John's smile faded a little. His mother had started dating one of the Buttucci brothers after Cassie and John had competed in the home renovation contest last summer. "Fine. He's still in my good graces. But I swear, one false move..."

Andie smiled at his overprotective attitude toward his mom. Cassie patted his hand, and he resumed eating. Then her sister turned to her. "So tell us about your weekend."

What to say? "It was fine. No big deal."

Cassie glanced at the cast on Andie's wrist. "I've avoided the elephant in the room, but I'm going to ask. Did Beckett have something to do with your injury?"

"This?" Andie held up her wrist. "No, not at all. I fell on it."

"Fell?" Cassie's expression was instantly worried.

"A simple accident. Beckett would never hurt me." The thought of that made Andie want to laugh. And cry because she knew that he blamed her injury on himself. It had been her. All her. And yet, he seemed to think that he was responsible for everything that went wrong. That wasn't right.

"I know he's got some issues."

"PTSD."

Cassie nodded. "And it can make people do some things they normally wouldn't."

She paused and reached out to touch Andie's good hand. "So tell us what happened."

"I told you. I fell."

"There's more to it than what you're saying."

John stood, picking up his plate of pie. "If it would be easier to talk without me here, I can give you two some privacy."

Andie waved off his suggestion. "We don't need privacy because there's nothing to share."

John balanced his mug of coffee on the plate. "Still, I think I'll give you two a moment. Besides, I want to check the news. Do you mind?"

The two sisters were left sitting across from each other at the table as he walked into the living room and put on the television. Cassie removed her hand from Andie's. "What really happened? Because you seem a little sad."

"It's true that I fell." She couldn't share about why she'd fallen because she wouldn't, couldn't betray Beckett's own private demons. "But that's not why I'm morose."

"Uh-oh. You broke out a big word, so I know it's serious."

Andie smiled at her sister's glib response. "Something changed between Beckett and me over the weekend, and I'm irresolute about what to do."

"Something bad? Is that why you're morose? And what in the world does irresolute mean?"

"It means I haven't resolved what to do. I'm of two minds." She dragged her fork through the caramel. "Do I pursue the strong possibility of another fruitless relationship? Or do I honor his wishes to let this attraction subside?" She brought her gaze back to Cassie's. "Why are you smiling?"

"Because you always do this. You either pursue the guy who you think needs to be saved or the one who isn't interested. In Beckett's case, he's both." Cassie leaned back in her chair with a shrug. "It's like you're trying to resolve your issues with Daddy by making the guy love you."

Andie shook her head. "This has nothing to do with Daddy."

"Doesn't it? You've been trying to earn his love and respect since you were born."

"Just because you're his favorite doesn't mean you have some special insight into my relationship with him."

Cassie cocked her head to the side. "I know what I see. You work so hard to get his attention. And you do that in your relationships with men, as well. Do I have to bring up Brian?"

Andie shuddered and shook her head. "Brian has nothing to do with this. He was a big mistake. Huge. But I've learned my lesson." She'd tried to pursue a relationship with the man for five years, ignoring the attention of available men until she'd finally realized last year that it would never happen between them. Five years wasted on someone who had been only halfhearted in their relationship. Not that he had ever called it that. "Beckett at least notices me, even if he doesn't want to."

"But he doesn't want a relationship, right?"

"I don't think he knows what he wants."

"I'm telling you this is shades of Brian. But more important, it's about Daddy.

Don't you think it's time you found a relationship with someone who wants to be with you?" Cassie pushed her dessert plate away, leaving half of the slice of pie. "If I eat any more of this, I won't be able to fit into my wedding gown."

Andie pushed her own half-eaten piece of pie away from her, as well. She wasn't hungry anymore. Partly because she knew what Cassie said was true. Why was she even considering pursuing something with a guy who clearly didn't want to be with her? If Beckett wanted a relationship, he wouldn't push her away like he had. He didn't do relationships, he'd said. So what was there to debate?

Because you want him, her heart reminded her. And he wanted her too, even if he wouldn't admit it to himself. She was as sure of that as she was that she would need to let him go. Her heart couldn't handle another rejection.

BECKETT WROTE A check for the plumber and thanked him for his labor before returning to the kitchen. Work on the new house was going slow, but at least the house was starting to take shape. With the contest, he'd been given a specific family to build and design for which had given him focus. Here, he could make choices on what he liked and thought would sell. In some ways, that was more difficult.

A knock on the kitchen doorframe brought his focus to the present. He found Rob lounging in the doorway. "Miss me?"

Beckett smiled and gave Rob a few thumps on his shoulder. He looked down at the brace on Rob's knee. "Shouldn't you be home recuperating?"

"Doc said I needed to get around more, so here I am." Rob glanced at the kitchen and whistled. "You've got the cabinets up already? You sure didn't waste any time. Probably means you're working all hours and not taking care of yourself again."

Ignoring the censure in Rob's voice, Beckett pulled out a blue-gray tile that he'd chosen for the kitchen floor. "I've got a guy coming in next week to tile here and in the bathroom."

"It looks good."

"So do you." And despite Rob's knee in a brace, he looked as if he was there ready for work. His color looked much better than he had the last time Beckett had seen him. "Want to help me pull up carpet in the master bedroom?"

Rob gave a laugh, shaking his head. "Think I'll have to pass on that for the moment." He checked his watch. "I should go. Physical therapy appointment, but I wanted to stop in and see how things were going."

"Slower without you. But definitely much quieter." He followed Rob to the front door and saw Rob's mom sitting in the car in the driveway. He raised his hand in greeting and walked with her son to the car, opening the passenger door for him. He stuck his head into the car. "Good to see you, Mrs. Veenstra."

"Rob said he had to see the house."

"I'm glad he stopped by. It's not the same here without him." He turned to Rob. "If you need anything, call me. Rides to the doctor. Help with the medical bills. Whatever you need." He looked over at Mrs. Veenstra. "You, as well."

"Thanks, Lieutenant."

He waved as Mrs. Veenstra backed the

car out of the driveway. Seeing Rob had been good, but it reminded him of all that needed to be done before he could sell the house. Speaking of, he had carpet to tear out in the master bedroom.

Beckett grunted as he pulled up the dark green shag carpet and smiled at the hardwood floor beneath. Older houses like these tended to have hidden treasures, and the scratched maple wood was no exception. He'd have to sand and restain it, but the end result would be worth the effort.

Someone whistled from the doorway. He looked up to find Cassie nodding in appreciation of the hardwood floor. "They really don't make houses like they used to." She squatted down and ran a hand along the scarred surface. "What I would give to find this in my house."

This seemed to be the day for visitors. "How is your house coming?"

She gave a shrug. "You know how it is. You're more likely to work on someone else's house than have time for your own. But I promised John that we will finish it after the wedding."

Beckett nodded, remembering the wedding invitation that she'd sent him. Had he sent his regrets to her? A wedding with a bunch of people was the last place he needed to be. "Sorry I won't be there."

Cassie eyed him. "But I think you will be."

"And why is that?"

"Because Andie wants you there."

The mention of the woman who had occupied his thoughts the last two days brought up a fresh wave of pain. "Cass…"

She took a step inside the bedroom and pulled out a utility knife from her back pocket. "Let's get this carpet up first, then we'll talk. Deal?"

He jumped on the suggestion, and between the two of them they removed the carpet in short order. When the last piece had been placed into the dumpster in the driveway, Cassie dusted off her hands and glared at him. "I need to know what your intentions are toward my sister."

He gulped, unprepared for her direct statement. "I have no intentions."

She sighed. "That's what I figured." She shook her head. "And you've told her this?"

"Yes, I have."

"But…"

He held up his hands. "There is no but. I can't be in a relationship with Andie. And that's exactly what I told her Sunday."

"And yet, you can't stop thinking about her."

He raised an eyebrow at Cassie's assertion. "Are you reading my mind?"

"Listen. I know the effect my sister has on men. She's beautiful inside and out. Most men can't help falling for her. They flock to her like a moth to flame." She put her hands on her hips. "And yet they don't understand that she wants more than their appreciation. She wants their respect. And their love and affection."

He knew all of this, which is why he'd put distance between them on Sunday. "I don't think I can give her what she wants."

Cassie nodded. "Then hear me out on this. If that's truly how you feel, you need to let her go. Don't make an excuse to run into her somewhere. Don't call or text her. And don't come to my wedding. She's been hurt enough without you having to add to it, so stay away."

"I have no intention of hurting her."

"Good." She let out a big breath. "On the other hand, if there is a chance for the two of you, don't be stupid and let her slip away. She'd be good for you. Just make sure you know what you want before you go to her."

"You're protective of her."

"I'm her little sister. I have to be."

He gave a nod, hoping they could drop the topic. Would his little brother have been so protective of him if Beckett had given him the chance? "I've got to get back to this. Thanks for helping me with the carpet."

"My pleasure. I'd love to see the house when it's finished."

"And congratulations on your wedding."

"Thanks." She took a few steps then turned to look at him. "Really think about it though before you decide whether you're coming or not. Don't let fear keep you alone."

He watched her leave, considering her words. He wasn't afraid of being alone. That's what kept him safe. Protected.

He meant that's what kept others safe. And yet, maybe he'd gotten it right the first time. If he was alone, he wouldn't have to lose anyone else. Wouldn't have to grieve their loss.

He stopped for a long drink of water before he got back to work. Such thoughts were what his therapist hoped to hear, so maybe he would save the insights for her later that day at his appointment.

BECKETT STARED AT the tree outside the therapist's office and wished again that he could be anywhere but there. He'd never found comfort in unloading what was in his heart. *Keep it locked up.* Isn't that what his dad had always told him? And yet, his dad was the one who died from a massive heart attack at an early age.

Dr. Samples cleared her throat and tapped her finger on her notepad. "I'd like to hear what you think about that."

Beckett tried to focus, aware that he hadn't heard the question. What was more, the therapist knew he hadn't heard it either. He reached down and patted Phoebe, trying to buy some time. Finally, he looked up at the doctor and offered a weak grin. "Think about what?"

"You're not paying attention."

He shook his head. "No, ma'am."

"I asked what you thought about your training with Phoebe."

He quit petting the dog and gave a shrug. "Good, I guess." The therapist didn't say anything, but looked at him over the top of her glasses that rested on the end of her nose. He held up his hands. "We've been getting along fine."

"And the nightmares?"

They hadn't gone away like he'd hoped they would. He had figured that following the doctor's suggestion about getting Phoebe would change that. And yet... "They're still there."

"Are they worse?"

"No."

"More frequent?"

He paused and thought. "No."

"Has Phoebe been able to calm you from them?"

She had at first. She'd jumped on his bed and poked her cold nose on his chest until he woke up. But last Saturday had shown him how far from cured he really was. She hadn't been able to waken him from the nightmare, and Andie had ended up getting hurt trying to save him. "Not always."

The doctor wrote something on her notepad. "Have you been taking the meds?"

She'd prescribed him antianxiety medications over the last six months, but he didn't like how they clouded his thinking. How they made him feel as if he was swimming in a big glass bowl rather than truly living. He couldn't function on them, so he had stored them in the back of his medicine chest. "I told you I stopped taking them."

"During the day, yes. But these will help you sleep."

The meds only made his nightmares even stranger. They messed him up worse than forgoing them. He shook his head. "They don't."

"I can prescribe you—"

"No." The word came out sharp, and the dog at his feet snapped her head up to look at him. Phoebe stood. He gave her a reassuring pat, then said to the therapist, "No more drugs."

"Lieutenant, I understand how you feel

about them, but they are meant to help you with the very things you're complaining of."

She didn't get it. No one did. "They work just fine for some people, I get that, but not me."

The thought of feeling separated from reality made him shudder. He needed to be grounded in real life. "You wanted to meet with me once a week, so I show up for these sessions. You wanted me to get a dog. I got a dog. But I'm not going to spend the rest of my life on meds when I don't genuinely believe they'll do me any good. What would be the point?"

He stood and walked to the window, staring out at the tree again. He remembered how he'd climbed similar trees with his younger brother. The need to get higher, to touch the sky. If only he could get back to those days where things weren't so complicated. When dreams were sweet. And when you did what you were supposed to, and things got better. He was doing everything they told him, but nothing had changed.

He looked over at Dr. Samples. "You can't fix me, can you?"

The psychiatrist laid her pen and notebook on her lap. "It's not a matter of 'fixing' you. I'm trying to give you tools to cope and eventually heal."

"Tools." He shook his head. "As a contractor, I know all about tools, Doc. But I think I'm wasting my time here." He reached over to grab Phoebe's leash and his coat from the back of the chair he'd been sitting in. "Goodbye, Doc."

She followed him out of the office and down the hallway. "Beckett, we still have twenty minutes left in our session today."

He paused at the door that lead to the waiting room. "No. We're done here. Therapy is voluntary, right?"

"No one is forcing you to come to these appointments, Lieutenant, but it was recommended by your CO."

True, Beckett had been in a dark place after Ruggirello's death, but he wasn't about to harm himself or others. The fact that Rob and Andie had both gotten hurt while near him caused him enough pain.

Therapy couldn't change that. "Then you're fired."

"Lieutenant—"

"I'll keep the dog and train with her, but these weekly sessions are done."

"I wouldn't give up on our time here."

"Why not? You don't make me feel better. Nothing we've done in these visits has helped me."

"So what does?"

CHAPTER TEN

ANDIE RESTED HER cast on the edge of the worktable in Russ's basement. She wouldn't be any use cutting glass, but she could sort through the new glass and figure out which pieces could go where in the window. And if she was being honest with herself, she wanted to check in with Beckett, see how he was doing. Knowing he would show up to work on the window, she hadn't hesitated in coming despite her limitations.

Russ walked down the stairs and joined her at the table. "I just got off the phone with Beckett. He's not coming."

His words left her feeling deflated. She'd been so hopeful after work. Had gone home and changed into an outfit that looked casual, but also made her sparkle, she knew. She sighed and rose to her feet.

"Well, I'm not of much use tonight. Guess I'll go home."

"Take a seat, Andie."

She lifted her cast for him to see. "Russ, I can't use my hand to cut glass. And my sorting is almost done. There's no purpose for me to stay."

The older man gave her a look and pointed at the stool she'd just vacated. "Sit." She obeyed his command, and he took the stool next to hers. "What are your objectives when it comes to Beckett?"

She frowned at his question. "Excuse me?"

"I have eyes. I see how you look at each other. So, what are your intentions?"

She felt the blush start to burn in her cheeks, and she dropped her gaze to her hands that rested in her lap. "I don't see how that is any of your concern." She looked up at him. "No offense."

"None taken." He stood and took a picture off the wall before returning to his seat. "You know my history as a Vietnam vet."

She took the picture from him and nodded. "You've shared some stories with me about your time there."

"I never told you what it was like to come home, did I?"

"You and Mrs. Thorpe started your family, and you opened the glass store."

Russ pointed at the picture. "Does anything about me in that picture remind you of someone?"

Andie looked down at the picture. Russ stood next to a younger version of Mrs. Thorpe, who held a baby in her arms. While she beamed in the photograph, there was a different look in Russ's eyes. She'd seen that same vacant expression on Beckett's face more than once. And while Russ stood near his wife, there seemed to be a distance between them. They didn't touch. "You don't look very happy."

"I wasn't. Not for a long time." He took the picture back and returned it to its place on the wall. "I didn't want to be a husband or a father then. I wanted to forget. To disappear."

"And you're saying Beckett feels the same way?"

"Beckett canceled tonight because he knew you would be here."

The words hit like arrows striking her

chest. She closed her eyes to keep the hot tears from falling. Beckett not only didn't want a relationship, but he didn't want to see her at all? What had she done that had been so horrible? "I don't understand what I'm doing that is so wrong."

"When I came home from the war, just being in the same room with Pattie made me feel itchy. Like I needed to escape. Because being around her made me feel things. And that's the absolutely last thing I wanted."

"And that's how I affect Beckett? I make him feel things he wants to forget?"

Russ gave a shrug. "I'm no doctor, but what I do know is that Beckett is struggling with some things."

"And so I should stay away from him."

Russ took a seat next to her and leaned closer. "No, you shouldn't. You're good for him whether he realizes it or not."

Andie cocked her head to the side, confused about this conversation. She thought Russ had been warning her away from Beckett. "So you think I should pursue him even though he doesn't want a relationship with me?"

Russ scooted forward on his stool and took Andie's good hand in one of his. "You're probably better off talking to my lovely wife on that count. She can tell you what she went through to bring me back. But what I can say is that if you have the feelings for him that I believe you do, then don't you give up on him." He gave her a hard look. "But you better make sure you know what your feelings are before you approach him."

That was the big question. She knew she was attracted to the man, but did her feelings go deeper? Could they deepen into a lasting relationship? And how would she know if Beckett showed no signs of wanting a relationship with her? Maybe Cassie was right. She did have a tendency to fall for the unavailable man.

When it worked out though, it made the victory even sweeter.

Unfortunately, the victories were rare.

BECKETT DREW THE glass cutter straight toward him, pressing it firmly in place. Once he had reached the edge, he dropped the cutter beside him on the worktable and tapped the glass. It broke off with a clean line. He looked up at Russ and smiled. "It worked."

"Of course, it worked. I'm not teaching you techniques that fail." He nudged the practice piece of glass closer to Beckett. "Do two more straight edges, then I'll show you how to make curves."

Beckett nodded and concentrated on cutting along the marked line on the glass. A noise above them broke his concentration, and his line slanted off the mark. He muffled a curse and placed the cutter on the table. "I messed that one up."

"You need to focus on the cutter and the glass. Nothing else matters."

He glanced up at the ceiling. "You don't think it's Andie, do you?"

"It's probably a friend of Pattie's or a neighbor stopping by. Now concentrate." He tapped the table.

Beckett nodded and looked at the mark, oiled the edge of the cutter and placed it against the glass. Scored it perfectly along the line. Russ patted him on the back. "Good."

Footsteps above drew Beckett's attention back to the ceiling. "You asked her not to come, right?"

"With her cast, she wouldn't be much help."

Beckett gave him a look that he hoped proved how serious he was. "You didn't answer my question."

Russ stared at him for a long moment. "You ever try telling a woman what to do? Doesn't work too well, in my experience."

"I can't concentrate if I think Andie's going to show up at any moment."

"And why is that?"

Beckett scowled and stared at the mark on the glass. Oiled the cutter. Pressed it firmly on the glass and scored a straight line. He had to prove that he could put Andie out of his mind.

And yet, she had never left it. Not since last weekend's road trip. In fact, she'd invaded his thoughts to the point where she had started showing up in his nightmares too. Now it wasn't just Ruggirello he had to save, but her too. And those nightmares scared him the most.

He left the cutter on the worktable and took a step away. Walked to the washtub by the washing machine and turned the water on. He cupped the cool water into his hands and splashed his face with it. When had it gotten so hot down here? He turned to find Russ handing him a towel. He nodded in thanks and took it, patting his face with the soft cotton.

"You okay, son?"

"I just got too warm."

Russ considered him for a second, then walked back to the worktable. Beckett joined him there. "Show me how to do curves."

The older man shook his head. "You're not ready."

Beckett pointed at the cuts he'd already made. "I've done straight edges, now show me the curves."

"For that, your head needs to be clear and focused on the task at hand."

"It is." He threw the towel over one shoulder. "Russ, I can concentrate. Please."

Russ took a seat on a stool and crossed his arms over his chest. "Why don't we talk first? Maybe get Andie out of your head for a moment."

"Talking won't get her out."

"So you admit she is on your mind."

Caught, Beckett could only give a short nod. "More than before. So how do I get her out?"

Russ laughed at the idea, shaking his head at the idea's seeming absurdity. "You tell me how to get a woman off your mind, and we can make a mint teaching others."

"You've had this problem?"

"And still suffer from it." Russ patted him on the shoulders. "The day I don't think about Pattie is the day you bury me."

For some reason, that didn't reassure Beckett. "But I don't want to think about her. Nothing good can come from it."

"You sure about that?"

Beckett ran a hand through his short hair rather than pulling it out like he'd first thought to do. "Yes. I can't love her."

"Whoa. You brought out the word *love* awfully quick."

Had he? He wasn't sure about anything anymore. "You know how it is. What can I bring to a relationship if I'm broken?"

"You're not broken, son. At least not beyond repair."

"You don't know that."

Russ raised an eyebrow. But Beckett knew what he knew. Nothing he tried would make himself whole again. Pieces of him had shattered and would never be fixed. Beckett tried to explain again. "You returned from war a changed man, so you understand what I'm talking about."

"And yet Pattie and I are still married."

"Happily?"

"Now, yes. But it took a while for us to get to this point."

"So you know what I'm saying." He snapped his fingers at Phoebe who approached him, and he took the leash in his hands.

Russ stood and pointed at the stool beside him. "Sit."

Phoebe rested on her backside, but Beckett remained standing. "If you're not going to teach me curved lines tonight, I think we should end it here. I'll be back in a few days."

"I said 'sit.' We're not done yet tonight."

Phoebe leaned into his leg, and Beckett thought about walking out despite the order, but finally took a seat on the stool. He looked at Russ who took a deep breath before starting his story. "When I got back from Nam, I thought everything would be okay. I was free. I was home. And Pattie was happy."

"But you weren't?"

"Who is telling this story?"

Beckett closed his mouth and waited for the older man to continue. "Pattie was happy and soon she was pregnant. I figured that a baby would solve what I was feeling. That I could forget everything that had happened and move forward.

"But when my son was born, the nightmares got worse. I started drinking more than I should. Pattie would cry and beg me to stop, but I couldn't. Nothing mattered to me but drinking to forget. Not Pattie. Not my son." Russ paused and rubbed his upper lip with one finger. "She threatened to leave me if I didn't get some help. But I knew better than she did. There was no help."

Beckett nodded at that. Nothing had helped his nightmares. Phoebe had helped wake him up during the worst of them, but they hadn't stopped. "What happened next?"

"Pattie took the baby and left. She filed for divorce, and I didn't do a thing to stop her. I just let my family slip out of my fingers, because I knew that they were better off without me."

Wait. Beckett looked toward the ceiling and shook his head. "I don't understand. You said that you and Pattie were still married."

"We are."

"She came back?"

"Not for a while." Russ let out a long breath. "Without Pattie, my drinking got even worse. I didn't think that was possible. I had just started the glass business, but there were days I didn't go in to work. I was losing money hand over fist, but I didn't care. If I stayed drunk, I couldn't think or feel. And that was more important.

"I lost the business. Lost the house. I lived in my car until it got impounded, and I didn't have the money to get it out. So I lived on the streets, but I didn't care."

Russ started to get choked up, and he paused his story to wipe his eyes. "And then a buddy who had served in Nam with me showed up one day. He'd heard from Pattie about how far I'd sunk and found me sleeping on a park bench. And he told me what I'm about to tell you." Russ stood and poked Beckett in the chest. "A soldier never forgets what happened. But if you let it stop you from living the life you deserve, then the enemy has beaten you."

The older man took another deep breath. "After what they did to me in that POW camp, I was never going to let those sons of a gun win. So I got clean. I got sober. And then I worked on winning back Pattie's love. Because she was the best thing in my life."

Beckett cleared his throat, moved by the story. "How long did it take to win her back?"

"Son, I still work every day to deserve her love." Russ put a hand on Beckett's shoulder.

"What does your story have to do with Andie?"

"Because you're letting the enemy keep you from something you deserve. Do you really want them to have that power?"

No, he didn't. They had already taken

too much from him. Fellow soldiers. Ruggirello. Sleep. They didn't deserve to win
anything else from him.

"So what are you going to do about
Andie now?"

ANDIE MOVED BETWEEN the tables as her
young art students bent their heads over
their drawings. With Valentine's Day ap-
proaching in the next couple of weeks, she
had given them an assignment to draw
what they loved the most. Some drew pictures of family. Others of a pet. One boy
furiously colored his drawing of a large
plate of tacos. She patted him on his shoulder before moving to the next student.

"Miss Lowman?" Nellie in the back of
the room raised her hand. "If we finish
early, can we draw a second picture?"

Andie smiled and nodded, knowing that
her favorite artist would not only finish
her current picture but start a second and
third for later. She had a feeling that art
helped the shy young girl build up her confidence. "I have extra paper just in case."

A knock on the door brought her attention from the class to the arrival of a

visitor. The sight of Beckett filling the doorway brought her up short. Her heart thumped so loudly, she was sure the kids could hear it. She turned back to the class. "Everyone keep working on your drawing, and I'll be right back."

She walked out to the hallway where Beckett stood with Phoebe at his side, but kept the door open just in case her class needed her. "Beckett, I wasn't expecting you."

He brought out a large bouquet of white, red and dark purple peonies from behind his back. She accepted it and pressed her nose into the fragrant blossoms. "Thank you. They're beautiful."

"Their beauty pales compared to yours."

She brought her eyes up to meet his. "Why are you here?"

He stayed silent and for a moment she tried to come up with the reasons why. Had he changed his mind about her? He glanced at the cast on her wrist. "I came to apologize."

"For what?" For her injury? It hadn't been his fault. Or for pushing her away? When he didn't expand on it, she figured the flowers were a guilt offering. She gave a short nod. "I need to get back to my class."

She started to walk inside when he called her name. She turned, and he reached for her free hand. "I'm not good with words like you are."

"What do you want, Beckett?"

"I want you to come back and work on the window with me."

His words did nothing to ease the ache in her chest. She held up her arm with the cast. "I can't exactly help with anything right now."

"I know, but just having you there makes a difference." He stared at his feet, and when he spoke it came out in a whisper. "I've missed you."

This soft-spoken admission warmed her heart. "I've missed you too."

A commotion from the class captured the attention of them both. She pointed toward the room. "I need to get in there before they stage a coup."

"Could I see you later?"

He could see her every day if he wanted.

She offered a small grin. "I'm teaching until three today."

He glanced at his watch. "How about grabbing some dinner before we go work on the window? I could pick you up at your apartment about five."

It almost sounded like a date. "Five o'clock." She waved and watched him turn and leave.

When she returned to the classroom, she was met by whistles and cheers. A boy near the back raised his hand. "Are you going to draw your boyfriend?"

BECKETT HADN'T PLANNED on waiting for a table, and being in a public place where so much could go wrong made him antsy. Itchy. Russ had nailed it when he'd used that word to describe the feeling that he couldn't set aside. Ants seemed to be walking up and down his spine, arms and legs. Phoebe walked beside him, turning when he did. Andie placed a hand on his arm. "It's okay. We can go eat somewhere else."

He glanced at her. This wasn't how he'd intended for the evening to go. He had figured they'd have a nice dinner with a place that had tablecloths, then go work on the window. He gave a nod, conceding that waiting wasn't going to help calm down his emotions.

They ended up at a small Italian pizzeria. When Andie walked through the door, the woman behind the counter exclaimed something in Italian and came around to kiss her on both cheeks. "*Bella cara*, how is your mother?"

"She's doing as well as can be expected. Cassie's wedding is coming up, so she's been more high-strung than usual."

The woman glanced at Beckett and narrowed her eyes. "You're the one who beat our Cassie in that contest." She glanced at Andie. "Consorting with the enemy?"

"He's a good man who beat Cassie fair and square."

The woman gave a harrumph of disbelief, then looked him up and down. "Are you hungry?"

He gave a nod as Andie answered for them, "We're famished, Lucille."

The woman smiled widely at her and waved her hand at a few empty chairs.

"Go ahead and take a seat. I'll make you our best for your dinner."

Beckett eyed Andie as she took a seat in one of the chairs. "We're not ordering dinner for ourselves?"

"Lucille will make us an unbelievable feast. You won't know how good until we take it home." She rested her hand on his as he claimed the seat next to hers. "Trust me. My family has known Lucille and Sal since I was a baby."

He liked the feeling of her hand on his, and when she started to remove it, he grasped her fingers in his. "The crazy thing is that I do trust you."

Andie smiled back at him, seemingly pleased with his words. "Lucille has been known to hold on to a grudge, so don't take her reaction to you too seriously. She's very loyal to Cassie."

"I could tell."

Andie appeared to be studying him and considering her words. "There's something I've been wondering. Why did you enter that contest? You don't like attention, and yet you risked winning and gaining national recognition. Was it the money?"

"Part of it. After I split the winnings with the decorator, I used my share to hire a buddy of mine who needed a job, then expand my business."

"And the other part?"

"That's harder to explain."

Andie glanced around the restaurant. "We've got time before our dinner is ready."

He stayed silent, watching her. If he could trust her with the smaller things, he could trust her with this too. Finally, he sighed and gave a shrug. "A good friend of mine died, and I thought the contest would help me work through my grief."

"And did it?"

He shook his head. "I missed Ruggirello all the more because he wasn't there to see it."

Andie put her hand in his. "I'm sorry."

He reached up and tucked her hair behind her ear. "It's not your fault."

"Still, I'm sorry that you lost your friend."

As if sensing his discomfort, she changed the topic and they talked about the window. He shared how he'd learned to make straight cuts, but not the curved ones. Andie gave his hand a quick squeeze. "My guess is that Russ will have us practice the easier pieces first before tackling the harder curved sections. But if you can make those straight cuts, the curved ones will come after a while."

"How much longer do we have for me to be practicing when we should be finishing this window?"

Andie smirked at this. "Are we on a deadline now?"

"Pattie told me that she's almost convinced Russ to go on that cruise. I'd like to finish the window before they go."

"That could be months."

"Or a few weeks." From the sound of things, Russ was ready to go along with his wife's plans.

They sat for a moment as tantalizing aromas drifted out to them from the kitchen. Her belly grumbled, and she winced, putting a hand on her stomach. "Sorry about that."

"You don't have to apologize. I'm hungry too." He stared at her. "I feel like I'm the one who needs to apologize."

She sighed and put her wrist with the cast in her lap. "I told you. It was my own fault for breaking my wrist. If I had waited—"

"I meant about my first impression of you. I assumed that you couldn't help me with the window, and I treated you rather harshly." He winced at the memory. "I'm sorry for being such a jerk to you."

"You weren't." He raised one eyebrow at this until she blushed and gave a short nod. "Okay, so maybe you were. But you've been nothing but a gentleman since."

"I'm not good with people."

"You're better than you think. In fact, you see yourself much more flawed than you really are."

"You sound like my therapist."

"Is that such a bad thing? You're so hard on yourself, but let me tell you what I see when I look at you." She reached over and placed a hand on his cheek. "I see a man who has lived a hard life, but still strives to find beauty. You are a hero with scars, sure, but still a man who is noble and—"

"Andie, stop. Please." He backed away, and she dropped her hand to her lap.

"I was only trying to tell you—"

"I know what you were trying, but believe me when I say those kinds of words don't make me feel better."

She brought her gaze up to meet his. "I don't understand. Why not?"

"Because they're not true."

"But those words are how I feel about you."

He backed up his chair, the screech of the wooden legs on the tile floor echoing through the restaurant. "Maybe this was a bad idea."

"Beckett, don't leave. You were doing fine."

He looked over at her and then reached down to pat Phoebe, who had started to rub her snout on his leg. "It's okay. I'm good. But can we change the subject?"

Andie nodded, but didn't say another word until Lucille brought out their dinners packed in cardboard boxes and waved off Beckett's money. "You treat our Andromeda well. That is payment enough."

BACK AT ANDIE'S APARTMENT, she set the table with plates and silverware she pulled out of cupboards as he unpacked the food. In one of the bags, he discovered an antipasto salad with small plastic tubs of homemade Italian dressing. He opened the large box, and the smell of garlic and cheese made his nose twitch appreciatively and his stomach growl in anticipation. The pizza was followed by a container of spaghetti and meatballs topped with melted parmesan cheese and another of breadsticks stuffed with melted mozzarella. Beckett took one and bit into it. He almost moaned in delight.

Andie smiled. "I told you it would be good."

Dinner held a calm atmosphere as they filled their plates, and conversation turned to the food and the work on the window that still waited for them. The knot in Beckett's belly loosened, and he realized that his life could be more like this if he would stop pushing good things away. He could let go of the tension that seemed to surround him. This wasn't Iraq where danger could come from any direction.

"Cassie's wedding is next Saturday."

Beckett brought his gaze up to Andie's

who looked at him with expectation. He grabbed his glass of water and took several gulps before he gave her a nod. "Yes, it is."

She seemed to be waiting for him to say something. He glanced away for a moment, trying to buy some time to figure out what to tell her. When he brought his focus back to Andie, her eyes appeared a little sad. "You're not going, are you?"

"I don't know yet."

"Cassie would want you to be there."

"Actually, she told me not to come if it would hurt you. That it would be better if I stayed away."

He hadn't meant to tell her that, but it was out there now. Andie twisted her napkin in her hands. "She doesn't get to decide that for you."

He glanced over her shoulder at the flowers he'd given her earlier. She'd arranged the blooms in a vase. He had wanted to see her, to apologize for how she had gotten hurt. Staying away from her seemed to hurt her even more though, than being near her. And yet, sitting here eating dinner with her, he mentally counted down the minutes until he could leave.

He placed his napkin beside his plate. "We should get ready to go soon to work on the window. I'll help you clean up." He got to his feet.

She rose out of her chair. "Wait. There's ice cream in the freezer for dessert."

He raised an eyebrow at this. "You think I'm here just for food?"

"Why are you here?"

She watched him so closely, and he felt like fidgeting under her gaze. "I wanted to apologize."

"You said that earlier."

This woman wasn't going to make it easy on him, was she? "I like being around you, but I'm afraid that I'm leading you on."

"Where are you leading me?"

"I can only give you friendship."

Andie bit her lip, her eyebrows furrowed into a frown. "Friendship."

"But you want more than that." He stated it as truth since he could see in her eyes that the idea of friendship wasn't enough for her.

"You don't know what I want."

"A woman like you always wants more."

Andie straightened at his words. "A woman like me?"

"You told me earlier what kind of man I was, so let me tell you what I see when I look at you." He walked around the table and put a hand on her cheek. "I see a woman who is beautiful. Smart and talented. Kind. Compassionate. A woman who deserves to be loved completely by a man." He dropped his hand. "But I'm not that man."

Andie's lips trembled, but her eyes stayed dry. "Maybe not today, but one day soon?"

The last word came out as a question, one that he couldn't answer at that moment. "I don't know if I can ever be."

She took a deep breath as she massaged her forehead with one hand. "I don't think I should go tonight to help with the window. I've developed a headache."

"Andie—"

She looked up at him. "I wouldn't be of any assistance. And I need to ruminate on what you've said."

AFTER SEVERAL ATTEMPTS to make curved cuts into the glass, Beckett tossed the cutter on the counter. "I can't do this."

Russ propped his glasses on his forehead and stared at him hard. "You're giving up way too quickly, son."

"I keep trying to do what you said, but I'm messing it all up." He hit his elbow against the table. "I should just quit."

Beckett stood and stalked across the basement floor to the foot of the stairs. Phoebe joined him there, but he didn't ascend. Couldn't. Because deep down he knew this wasn't about cutting the glass. He turned to face Russ. "I apologize. I'm in a mood."

"I noticed."

Russ rose and approached him, but Beckett took a few steps back. "Maybe I should take the dog for a walk and clear my head."

"You'll still be thinking about her."

Beckett looked at the dog. "Phoebe?"

Russ cocked his head to the side. "Is that who you've been obsessing about since you got here this evening? And don't tell me you're not because I notice that she didn't come with you."

"I'm not obsessing."

Russ gave a shrug. "Fine. Enjoy your walk. But if you don't come back with a clear head, then our lesson is over tonight."

"Fine." Beckett plodded up the stairs with Phoebe leading the way. He fixed her leash to the collar and grabbed his coat. When he zipped it up, he noticed that Pattie sat on the couch in the living room with a ball of yarn, making what looked like the start of a blanket. He gave her a nod. "I'm taking Phoebe for a walk, but I'll be right back."

The dog gave a sharp bark to indicate her agreement with his plans. Pattie gave him a wave. "I'll make some hot chocolate for when you return."

He thanked her and headed out into the cold air. He pulled the collar of his coat higher to block the frigid wind. Maybe he should have brought his hat but he hadn't expected to be taking the dog for a walk while at Russ's house. And why was he? The dog seemed interested in sniffing snowbanks and ice patches, but little else.

He was here because he'd hoped to make amends with Andie, but had made an even bigger mess. He should have just kept his mouth shut. Kept his reservations and fears to himself. If he had, she'd be with him now. She'd probably cling to his arm as they walked, making jokes about how cold it was. And he'd feel a lot warmer than he did walking alone.

He kicked at a mound of snow, and Phoebe yelped as pieces of it crossed her path, startling her. "Sorry, girl. But I messed up big-time tonight."

She glanced back at him, and he waved apologetically. "Maybe I should have taken you with us on the date. Maybe you could have given me a signal when my mouth started getting me into trouble."

But if he had stayed silent about his doubts and worries, was that fair to Andie? It was like he'd said. She deserved a man who could give her everything, and Beckett wasn't that man. No, the truth was better.

The truth according to whom though?

He returned to the house, stamping the snow from his boots on the porch before entering the living room. Enticed by the smell of chocolate, he entered the kitchen and found Pattie and Russ talking quietly, but their conversation ended when he got closer. Pattie smiled at him as she handed him a mug full of cocoa. "Why don't you take a seat, Beckett?"

Receiving his own mug, Russ kissed his wife and headed back to the basement. Beckett watched his retreat and thought of following him. But Pattie insisted he stay.

"Thank you for the hot chocolate, ma'am. It's pretty cold out there."

She eyed him for a moment, then leaned against the edge of the kitchen sink. "Why didn't Andie come tonight?"

"I told you, she had a headache."

"So you did."

Pattie continued to watch him, so he took a sip of the cocoa and winced as it burned his tongue. Before the next sip, he blew on it. Anything to stall for time since

Mrs. Thorpe seemed to want him to talk. And he didn't know what to say.

Finally, she took a seat across from him at the table. "She loves you, you know."

He shook his head. She couldn't love him, because she didn't really know the truth about him. And if she did, she wouldn't have anything to do with him. "She only thinks she does."

"Russ told me the same thing when he first came back from Vietnam."

Beckett started to stand. "Mrs. Thorpe, I don't think—"

"Sit."

"But I don't need to hear about how Russ hurt you for years. I know that story."

She kept her eyes on him, and he slowly slipped back into the chair. Once he was seated and watching her, she smiled at him. "You know Russ's side of how things happened. And I'm sure that you identified with what he said because the two of you are so much alike. More than you'd care to admit, most likely."

Beckett played with the handle of the mug, turning it first one way, then the other. "We've both been in combat situations, so we can appreciate what it's like to come home."

"That's the thing. I don't think you're really home yet."

The nightmares he had seemed to agree with her. Part of him had stayed in Iraq, and he didn't know how or even if he could be whole again. "No, ma'am. Which is why Andie deserves better."

"Yes, she does. But that doesn't mean she doesn't deserve you." Pattie put her hands on the tabletop as if trying to appeal to him. "Beckett, the things you saw and what you did overseas is not you."

"You don't know what I did."

"Not specifically, but I do know what was required of Russ to survive. The friends he lost. The men he killed." She paused. "For years, he called himself a murderer. It's why he drank."

Tears sprang to Beckett's eyes, and he had to glance away. It was as if she could see inside his head. "You don't—" His voice broke, so he cleared his throat before continuing. "You don't know what it's like to see the light go dim in the eyes of the one you killed."

"Did you have a choice?"

There was always a choice, but it had come down to either his life or theirs. And he'd fought to be the victor. "We were taking heavy fire from insurgents on a rooftop. If I didn't take out the snipers, I'd lose my men, and that was not an option." He ran a hand through his hair, wanting to forget but knowing he'd see the kid's face in his dreams later. "The shooter I killed couldn't have been more than sixteen. His little sister called me a murderer.

"They're both a part of my nightmares." His face. Her voice. Beckett closed his eyes and covered them with his hands. "I can't escape it."

"You are not a murderer. You are a good man."

He peeked from between his fingers at Pattie. "But I'm not."

"Yes, you are. You've just forgotten that part of you." She rose and walked over to stand beside his chair. "Who went above and beyond to win the house renovation contest to provide a home for a deserving family? And then who used the prize money to hire a fellow veteran?"

When he didn't answer, she continued, "Who cared for Andie when she hurt her wrist, rushing her to the hospital? Who brought me a gift when he barely knew me? And who has brought a purpose and a spark to my Russ as he retires?

"Don't tell me you're not a good man." She placed a hand on his back. "And you deserve the love of a good woman like Andie."

The tears he kept back started to choke him, and he coughed. Could she be right?

"Don't let a chance like this pass you by."

CHAPTER ELEVEN

ANDIE FUSSED WITH the hem of Cassie's wedding gown. Never one to play princess or dress up very girly, her sister made a beautiful bride in the floor-length silk shantung mermaid-style dress. It clung to Cassie's curves until it hit her knees, then flared out to the floor.

Cassie pulled the dress away from one hip. "Ugh, when can I change out of this?"

"Let's get you married first. Where are your shoes?" Andie glanced around the room and found the empty box where they should have been. Despite Andie's protests, Cassie had chosen to wear ballet flats instead of the heels that she'd found online. At least that was an upgrade to the tennis shoes her sister had chosen first.

"I put them on already. Sheesh. Calm down. You'd think you were the one getting hitched."

Andie pressed a hand to her chest, trying to calm the erratic beat of her heart. Her sister was right. She'd pass out if she kept up at this pace. "I only want things to be perfect for you."

"They already are with John waiting for me at the end of the aisle. So relax." Cassie looked at herself in the floor-length mirror, a soft smile playing around her lips. "I look hot. He's going to faint when he sees me."

Andie had to agree. She smoothed the sapphire blue satin of her own tea-length dress, then ran her left hand along the back of her head, checking for stray hairs that might have escaped the high bun. Why was she so nervous? Part of it was because she did want things to be perfect for Cassie, but another part wondered if Beckett would show up after all, although they hadn't left things on a good note last week. Would he think she looked hot and faint too? Would he see her and change his mind about keeping distance between them?

Cassie turned to look at her. "What's wrong?"

Andie waved off her question. This was Cassie's day, and she wasn't going to allow melancholy thoughts about Beckett to ruin it for her sister. "It's nothing."

"Give me a break. You've been moping all morning."

"I'm fine. And I'm not moping."

"Liar."

Andie glared at her sister. "Why don't you stay focused on getting through the ceremony and stop worrying about me?"

"Because I want you to be as happy as I am." Cassie walked toward her, the dress rustling with each step. "It's Beckett, right?"

"Like I said, it's nothing." He had made that very clear.

A knock on the door brought both sisters to attention. Andie answered it to find their mother dressed in a soft gray sheath dress, her hair coiffed into soft waves around her face. "We have about ten minutes left, girls." Their mother sighed at the sight of Cassie. "Oh, Cassandra. You're beautiful."

"Now I know what it feels like to be

Andie, if only for a day." Cassie winked at her sister.

"You're definitely outshining me today." She handed the simple but elegant bouquet of white roses to Cassie. "You ready for this?"

"I've been ready since he asked me to marry him."

Andie fussed again with the hem, trying to get it to lay flat on the floor. Cassie scolded her. "It's fine."

Another knock on the door. Aunt Sylvie poked her head inside the room. "They're starting the music for you."

Andie held out her arm. "Let's get you married."

"Finally."

When the wedding march began, Andie and her mother flanked Cassie at the back of the church. They were about to walk down the aisle, but Cassie put out her hand to stop Andie. "Wait for it."

At the front of the church, John turned and gaped at them. He shook his head and wiped at his eyes. Cassie smiled brighter, then nodded. "Okay. Now."

The service passed in a blur for Andie.

It seemed as if they'd just reached the front of the church before the priest announced the couple as husband and wife. Then the recessional rang out, and they were walking back down the aisle and forming a reception line at the doors to the church. Guests streamed past Andie, complimenting her, but eager to get to the happy couple with their congratulations.

She had endured a bone-crushing hug from one of John's uncles when she heard her name spoken by the voice that had been haunting her dreams. She found Beckett's piercing blue eyes on her. Her breath caught in her throat. While he was handsome already, he became stunning in a gray suit with an ice-blue tie that matched the color of his eyes. "I didn't think you were coming," she told him.

"I wasn't sure if I could." He didn't move, staring at her, then he took a step toward her. "You're dazzling in that dress."

He hadn't fainted, but she felt as if she'd won something from his admission. She reached out her left hand toward him. "Thank you for coming to the wedding. I know Cassie will be pleased."

He put his warm hand in hers, and Andie jerked at the sparks that his touch sent along her body. *Yes, more of this please*, her heart seemed to whisper. She kept her hand in his, staring into those eyes. If only she could keep him here.

"What about you? Are you happy that I came?"

She blinked several times. Should she tell him that she had ached at his absence? That she longed to be in the same room with him if only for just a moment. "Very."

A smile formed on his face. "Maybe you can save a dance for me later."

"I'd like that."

He removed his hand from hers, and she felt the warmth go with him. She kept her gaze on him as he approached Cassie and John. "Who was that handsome young man?"

Andie turned to Aunt Sylvie. "A friend."

"If a friend of mine looked at me like he looks at you, I wouldn't be single any-more." Aunt Sylvie smirked at her. "Does your mother know?"

Andie shook her head. "There's nothing

to know. We're just friends." And sometimes, she wondered if they were even that.

BECKETT SEARCHED THE banquet hall to find the table where he had been assigned to sit for the wedding reception. Coming to the wedding without Phoebe had been a risk, but he wasn't sure that bringing a dog would have been appropriate despite the fact that she was meant for his well-being.

His assigned table was on the periphery of the ballroom, so he sighed in relief and took a seat next to the wall so that he could visually scan the room. He also had a good view of the head table where Andie would be seated, and he liked the idea of being able to watch her from afar. Getting too close to her tended to make things messy in his mind. For the last week, he had struggled with the decision to come to the wedding. In the end, he had wanted to see her more than he wanted to stay away.

Several people approached the table, spotted the number displayed on the silver holder, then walked on. If he sat alone, he wouldn't have minded at all. But that thought was squashed by the arrival of a couple who gave him smiles before taking seats across the table from him.

The DJ played soft music as more people gathered in the hall. He figured there had to be about a hundred or so guests. Hopefully, they'd serve dinner soon, then start the dancing so he could make his excuses and leave. He'd made his appearance, placed his wedding gift envelope in the box with the others, and would dance with Andie one time. Then he could check off his duty as being done to Cassie and John as their guest.

The music became louder as the DJ announced the arrival of the new Mr. and Mrs. Robison. The newly married couple entered to applause with a few whistles. Beckett watched as Andie walked to the head table, turning and laughing at something the best man said. She looked amazing in that blue dress that clung in all the right places. And the way she had one long curl fall from the high bun to accentuate the curve of her neck. She sparkled. Why would she waste her time on a damaged guy like him when she could be happy with a guy like that?

The wedding party soon made their way through the buffet line, and tables were sent one at a time after that. Good. This wedding was moving right along. He could eat. Congratulate the couple. And make it home by nine to see the end of the basketball game.

Beckett's table was invited to come up to the buffet, and he had to pass by the wedding party on his way there. He found his mouth watering at the sight of Andie instead of the food, however. How could one woman look so appetizing? He shook his head. He had to get that idea out of his mind. Despite Russ's belief that Beckett deserved a good life, Beckett doubted that Andie was a part of it. She needed someone else, like the best man who flirted with her so easily. She laughed at something else the man said, and Beckett wondered if he had ever made her laugh like that. Dark fingers of jealousy twisted around his heart.

He took a plate and started to fill it with food, keeping his focus there rather than on the sight of Andie. Someone bumped into him and the plate crashed to the floor. He winced and bent to clean the mess.

A waiter approached him. "Here. Let me get that, sir."

Beckett glanced up at the man and nodded. "Sorry."

"Happens every night. Don't worry about it."

Beckett straightened and found that Andie was looking in his direction. He couldn't seem to take his eyes off her, couldn't move until the waiter handed him a clean plate.

He got back into the buffet line and had almost made it to the end when Andie walked up to him, her perfect brow marred with a frown. "Are you all right?"

He said nothing, but nodded. She put a hand on his arm before he could return to his seat. "I hope you'll save a dance for me later."

He wanted nothing more than to have her in his arms one last time. "I'm looking forward to it."

Someone called her name, but she gave him a dazzling smile before moving in the direction of the person who had called to her. He hated that she had to leave him so quickly. Hated that he hadn't thought of a reason to keep her by his side for just a minute more. Hated even more that he knew that nothing could happen between them. Not when she deserved so much more than he could give her.

ANDIE STOOD AS she tapped a knife on her champagne flute. The DJ brought over a microphone, and she smiled at him before taking it. She scanned the crowd first as she had learned in high school speech class, then picked up her note cards. "Thank you all for coming tonight to celebrate Cassie and John's marriage. Because even though the evening is well under way, they are at the beginning of a lifetime journey together. And that's definitely worth celebrating."

She scanned the crowd again and spotted Beckett sitting at a table near the back. The words she'd prepared to say slipped from her mind, and she fumbled with the cards to find where she'd left off. Looked up again and found Beckett. "The kind of love that Cassie and John share is special.

There's so much that can come between two people, and choosing to love, despite the obstacles, despite the issues they might have is an admirable feat.

"That's why we're here tonight. Two people were lucky to have found in each other the one who makes their life better. Who brings joy and happiness, safety and completion every day for the rest of their lives." She paused and picked up her glass of champagne. "Let's raise our glasses and toast Cassie and John. May their marriage be full of love, laughter and everything good that life can offer."

She faced Cassie and raised her glass a little higher before taking a sip of the fizzy champagne. When she sat back down, her sister reached over and hugged her. "Thank you," Cassie whispered in Andie's ear.

"Just be happy."

"I already am. Now it's your turn."

Andie handed the microphone to the best man who stood and started toasting the couple, as well. His words barely registered. She'd noticed that Beckett was still looking at her. Did he understand that she could choose him despite the issues they had? That she would like to find love with him that made her life more complete?

With the speeches done, Cassie and John cut the cake amid a group of guests taking pictures of them with their phones. And then the first dance was announced. John held out his hand to Cassie who rushed into his arms, smiling widely. Then Andie's name was announced with the best man's. He took her into his arms, but kept plenty of space between them. She didn't mind that since she only wanted to be in Beckett's arms.

When the DJ announced the next dance with Cassie and the Buttuccis, Andie stood on the edge of the crowd and watched as first Tiny, then Biggie led her sister around the room. It was the first moment she'd thought of her father all day. Even when she had been escorting her sister down the aisle, he hadn't come to mind. Her father had missed out on it all. And there was nothing he could do to make up for it. But Cassie didn't seem to mind as she rested her head against Biggie's chest as the big man let tears slip down his face.

After the mother-and-groom dance, the DJ turned up the volume and sped up the tempo of the next few songs. Guests gathered on the dance floor. Andie walked back to the head table and took a sip from her water glass.

"Andie."

She turned. Beckett was standing next to her. She reached out her left hand and straightened his tie, which had become askew, then patted it against his chest. "Did you come to ask me to dance?"

"I really can't dance, but yes I did."

She gave a shrug. "You seemed to do okay in the Thorpes' basement."

"There weren't a bunch of people watching us then." He gestured toward the busy dance floor. "I don't do well with crowds."

"So ignore them and keep your eyes on me."

He let out a sigh, as if her request was taxing on him, but grinned a little and took her hand. The fast music switched to a soft ballad, perfect for couples. She led him to the dance floor where she spotted Aunt Sylvie dancing with one of John's uncles, her head resting on the man's shoulder. Good for her aunt.

She turned to face Beckett as the music played. Finally, Beckett's hands gripped her hips and pulled her closer to his body. She put her arms on his shoulders and looked into his eyes while they swayed to the song. "You're doing fine."

His grin grew. "I liked your speech."

"I meant every word. Nothing should keep you from finding love."

He faltered in his steps and ended up on her toes. "Sorry." He hung his head to look at his feet.

She reached out and lifted his head to look at her. "It's okay. I like dancing with you. Just keep your focus on my eyes. Don't think about your feet."

His grip on her hips brought her a little closer, sending frissons of pleasure through her nerve endings. She wanted the song to go on and on. For this moment to stretch out forever if it meant she could be in Beckett's embrace just a little bit longer.

A loud thump, and the DJ's microphone sent out a jarring squeal interrupting the music. Suddenly Beckett had pulled Andie into a tight embrace, shielding her with his body against a presumed threat. His eyes darted around the room, and he breathed heavily. She put her hands on his cheeks. "Beckett, it's only the microphone. Look at me. Just breathe."

He looked back at her, and she nodded. "Breathe in." He obeyed. "Now let it out slow." Again, he complied. "One more time," she said.

She saw the panic starting to leave his eyes, but she kept her hands on his face. "You're okay."

He seemed to come back to himself then. "Sorry, Andie. I can't do this." He strode away from her.

She watched Beckett go, longing to run after him, but knowing that nothing she could say would change anything in that moment. Why couldn't he see that he was more than he thought? That he could be the hero of her dreams?

She felt her bottom lip tremble and reached up to still it. She wouldn't cry over Beckett. Not here at the wedding. She would wait until later once she was alone.

Alone. The word made her heart ache.

Still, there was a difference between alone and lonely. She might go home alone every night, but she was far from lonely.

"Cassandra's looking for you."

Andie turned and met her mother's gaze. "Thanks. I'll be there in a sec."

"Is there something going on between you and the young man that just left?" her mother asked, one silver eyebrow arched.

"No, Mother. He's just a friend."

Her mother sniffed, indicating what she thought of Andie's labeling Beckett as a friend. "Good. You don't need to be mixed up with him."

"What do you know about Beckett?"

"I've heard about him from your sister." She leaned closer to Andie. "You don't need another broken man in your life."

"He's not broken. Not like he thinks he is."

"Andromeda, when you were little you used to bring home birds with broken wings. Dogs and cats that had been abandoned or been hit by cars." Her mother gave her a smirk. "For a while, I figured you would become a veterinarian because you had such a heart for these hurt animals. But then, as you got older you started bringing home broken people. Friends who had been dumped, or whose parents had split up. Remember how you invited your teacher over to dinner, the one whose sister had passed? You have a huge heart for love, dear. But you can't save the world."

Andie bit her lip. Did she try to save everyone? Maybe she did, but why shouldn't she? She had a strong streak of compassion in her. Why should she apologize for that? Wasn't it worse to be otherwise? "Cassie says I pursue the unavailable guy."

"And I'd say this Beckett is the epitome of unavailability, don't you?"

"You don't even know him, Mother. Truth is, I only know a little about him, but what I do know makes me love him all the more."

Andie brought her hand to her mouth. Did she love him? Oh yes, she did. And the thought that he had walked out on her again made her sad. Maybe it was time for her to start saving herself, along with Beckett. "I have to go find Beckett before he leaves. Tell Cassie I'll be right there."

She picked up the hem of her dress and ran past her mother, determined to find Beckett because she was sure he'd found his excuse now to leave early.

She sidestepped a couple who were leaving the dance floor and scanned the exit doors. Choosing one, she ran out to the parking lot. Beckett was striding toward his truck parked at the end of an outer aisle. She called his name, but he didn't turn to look at her.

BECKETT LEFT THE banquet hall and took a wrong turn, winding up on a balcony that overlooked the street. He'd been enjoying the dance before he'd heard the crash, assumed that danger was near and crushed Andie to him. He'd been having fun, and his PTSD had taken that away from him. Was it always going to be this way? One day. He wanted just one day where he could be normal.

He pounded his fist on the balcony railing then returned to enter the hall. The doors to the parking lot weren't much farther, and he marched out of the wedding reception, heading for his truck. Within a few feet of its safety, he heard his name being called. He didn't have to turn around to know who it was.

He heard her footsteps and said to her, "It's cold out here, Andie. You should go back inside."

"I will when you do."

She'd freeze in minutes if she stayed outside with those bare arms. Sighing, he removed his suit coat and draped it over her shoulders. "Why did you follow me?"

"I wanted to make sure you were okay."

"Here's the thing. I'm never going to be okay. That's why you should stay away from me, Andie. I can't be fixed like some window that needs new glass. My scars won't heal."

He started to leave, but she grabbed his arm. "I don't accept that. Russ suffered from PTSD, and he's doing fine. Other soldiers do too."

"And some die."

"You're stronger than that."

"And what if I'm not? My best friend took his life because he wasn't as strong as he thought. He left a wife and two kids, Andie. I won't do that to my family."

She took a step away from him. "Have you thought of harming yourself?"

"There's no simple answer to that question."

"Sure there is. Yes or no?"

He took a long look at her and shook his head. "You don't want to be mixed up with me."

"Yes, I do. I'm falling for you, Beckett. And that means I want every part of you, scars and all."

Her words thrilled his heart as much as they filled his mind with dread. Standing before him was a woman whom he would one day hurt, and she deserved so much more than that.

Andie reached up, resting her hand against his cheek.

Heat from her hand seemed to radiate to his spine and down his back. He needed to let her go. Needed to walk away. "Andie—"

She put a finger on his lips. "Let me talk. I know all the reasons why you don't do relationships. But I also know the kind of man you are and that you have feelings for me too, even if you're not willing to admit it."

"No."

She nodded. "Yes, you do. And those feelings terrify you which is why you're rushing to leave me. I get it. I really do. But I'm strong enough to handle you and your scars."

He wasn't strong enough, so how could she be? "You don't know what you're saying."

"Then let me show you what I feel."

She pressed her lips to his, and he hesitated. He couldn't let this continue.

And yet as he grasped her by her upper arms to push her away, his lips betrayed him and deepened the kiss. He could feel her thread her fingers in his hair, and he wanted the moment to go on and on.

When he eventually broke the kiss and took a step back, he kept his hold on her. They were both breathing heavily, staring into each other's eyes. He knew he should let her go. Give in to his fear and walk away. But she took a step toward him and rested her head against his chest. He wrapped his arms around her and kissed the top of her head. "I don't know what to do with you."

"How about letting me in just a little?" She brought her head back to look into his eyes again. "Why don't we take it slow? Just one day at a time?"

He stared at her, gave a slight nod and brought her in for another toe-curling kiss that they would both dream of for weeks.

CHAPTER TWELVE

THE PATTERN OF the window lay before them on the worktable, pieces of cut glass positioned on the brown sheet. Andie sighed as she counted the number of empty spaces. Beckett had a good eye and steady hand when it came to cutting glass. If he kept this pace, they'd finish the window in no time. Despite his kisses at the wedding, she knew he'd still find a reason to quit their friendship.

She'd seen how uncomfortable her words had made him. The more tense he was, the farther he retreated from her. And that was the last thing she wanted.

"Andie, did you hear what I said?"

She blinked several times at Beckett. "Sorry. I wasn't paying attention. What do you need?"

"I asked you if you thought the wave pattern on the glass for the water should be left to right or top to bottom." He pointed to the piece of glass in front of him.

She gave the glass a glance. "Left to right. Waves go parallel to the shoreline, not perpendicular."

Beckett nodded and returned his focus to the pattern and glass cutter. Andie rubbed her forehead, then turned to Russ. "I'm getting a headache. Could I get some aspirin?"

"Sure. Go upstairs and ask Pattie. She'd be more than happy to give you some."

Andie left the two men and walked upstairs to find Pattie sitting in the living room with a ball of yarn and crochet hook. The older woman looked up and smiled at her as she entered the room. "Did you need something, dear?"

"Aspirin. Please."

Pattie set aside her crochet project and rose to her feet. She motioned for Andie to follow her down the hall to the bathroom where she opened a medicine cabinet and tapped two tablets into Andie's hand. She poured water into a tiny paper cup and handed that to her, as well. "I'm sorry you're not feeling well."

Andie took the medicine and crushed the cup before tossing it into the wastebasket. "Tension headache, I think."

Pattie glanced at her cast. "And I'm sure your injury isn't helping any."

Andie followed Pattie, who returned to the living room. She thought about going back down to the basement, but she couldn't help the window with this cast. And she needed some distance from Beckett to sort out her feelings.

Pattie motioned to the love seat next to her recliner. "You're welcome to sit and visit with me if you'd rather not return to the basement just yet."

Andie took a seat and looked at Pattie's crocheting. "What are you working on?"

Pattie laid the project out on her lap. "It's going to be a baby blanket once I finish. I knit about five or six over the long winter months, then donate them to a nearby shelter."

"You do beautiful work."

Pattie waved off her compliment. "I like to keep my hands busy, and now that I'm retired I have more time to devote to it."

"My grandmother tried to teach me

once when I was about seven, but I got more knots than actual stitches in the yarn." Andie reached over and fingered the soft pastel yarn. "I envy those who can do this."

"Once you get your cast off, I can show you some basic crochet stitches."

"I might take you up on that."

Pattie smiled and returned to working with the yarn. Andie watched her for a moment, then asked, "How did you and Russ deal with his PTSD when he came home from war?"

"Ah, I wondered when you would ask me." She kept her focus on the crochet hook and yarn, but Andie knew that her mind had traveled back to that time in their lives. "I can only tell you my side of things, but it wasn't easy on either of us." Her fingers stilled for a second, and she swallowed hard before continuing. "He drank to forget in those days, and he had a lot of forgetting to do." She looked up at Andie with moist eyes. "I told him it was either the alcohol or me."

"And he chose you?"

Pattie shook her head and continued

working the yarn. "Not at first. I left him and moved in with my mother. I figured Russ was going to drink himself to death, and I was afraid to watch him do it."

This didn't sound like the relationship she'd seen between Russ and Pattie. "You gave up on him?"

"He gave up on us, and I had a son to care for. I know it's probably hard for you to understand, but he had to decide to get better for himself. I couldn't nag him to do it. I couldn't plead or beg. They were just words."

"What made him change?"

Pattie set her crocheting aside. "He had to hit bottom. Homeless, jobless and alone. But he came back once he was sober. And he's been working so hard to make up for those lost years."

"Years?" Andie paled. Could she devote years of hoping to reach Beckett only to be turned away time and again? She'd done that with Brian, and she'd still ended up alone.

Pattie nodded. "When a soldier returns home from a war, it takes a long time to find peace. Russ did it. And I'm sure Beckett will too."

"I hope he does."

Pattie reached over and touched her hand. "You love him. I can see it in what you do and hear it in what you say. Russ has commented that you could be good for Beckett, but I want to give you a word of warning." She paused and looked square into Andie's eyes. "It won't be easy. There will be days you'll question why you're risking your heart. You'll wonder if it's worth the pain and anger, if you wouldn't be happier with someone else who doesn't come with these worries."

If the woman was trying to scare her off a relationship with Beckett, it certainly seemed to be effective. Could she be strong enough to love him, scars and all? Would she have the staying power when things got difficult?

And yet, the thought of turning her back on Beckett didn't seem possible. A future without him seemed bleak. He challenged her like no man had. And despite his protests, she knew that he could love her in the way she needed.

Pattie picked up her crochet hook and yarn and resumed her task. "If you love Beckett like I love my Russ, then it will be worth the struggle."

THE WEEKS PASSED in a blur of fixing up the house during the day and spending most evenings in the Thorpes' basement working on the stained glass window. Between Russ and himself, they had most of the pieces of glass cut. However, he and Andie still hadn't found the right amber glass for the light shining from the lighthouse. Russ had suggested some websites that might have the inventory they needed. Andie volunteered to track it down since she couldn't help cutting glass with her cast.

Despite being unable to help per se, Andie showed up most nights. She'd sit in a recliner with a cup of tea in her good hand, and Phoebe at her feet. The dog seemed to have bonded with her, and often rewarded her presence with doggy kisses that Andie protested about even as she giggled and smiled.

Beckett found himself looking forward

to those evenings. The friendships that had blossomed between them all brought a level of comfort he hadn't experienced since before Iraq. Restoring the window was important, of course, but the conversation and homemade desserts brought a sense of peace. The nightmares had become fewer. Panic attacks rare. Beckett felt so much better.

He had even found himself drawing emotionally closer to Andie. Since the wedding, she didn't push him for more than friendship and respected his need for space. He'd be cutting a piece of glass and look up to find her watching him. And he discovered he liked that.

Liked it so much that he had stopped her from following Russ upstairs when they had finished for the night. She frowned at him when he grabbed her hand. "What's wrong?"

"Nothing." He looked into her eyes and brought his hands up to frame her face before lowering his mouth to cover hers. She returned his kiss with a fire that both pleased and surprised him.

He tore his mouth from hers. "A friend

of mine is opening a restaurant next Saturday night. Come with me."

She nodded then rose on her toes to give him one more kiss that seemed to brand him with her name.

"Did you two get lost down there?" Russ called from upstairs.

Beckett let Andie go reluctantly. "I guess we should join them."

She stared briefly into his eyes before starting to walk past him up the stairs. He followed her to the kitchen where Pattie had set out that night's treat, a large bowl of fruit salad. Russ raised an eyebrow at this. "Really? Fruit?"

"Your doctor said you needed to watch your weight." Pattie set a small bowl of the fruit salad in front of him. "That means I'm changing what I feed you. And it starts with fruit. Watch it or I could get out the cottage cheese."

Russ scowled, but ate a strawberry.

Andie played with a blueberry. "I showed the pictures that I took of the window to one of my old professors. He said that something about it reminded him of another window he had seen before."

Beckett was intrgued. "Did he have an idea of who the artist was?"

"No, unfortunately. But he was going to do some digging and let me know if he discovered anything." She sighed and pushed her hair back away from her face. "I don't know why the identity of the artist is so important to me. Maybe because the creation of something that beautiful should be given proper credit. I'll keep looking if I have to."

"And if we never find out?" Russ asked.

"I'll widen my net." Andie speared a piece of pineapple. "There's something about the window that I feel I should recognize. Probably something I studied before. Like my professor, I just can't put my finger on it."

Beckett reached out and grabbed her free hand. "If anyone can figure it out, it will be you."

She returned his smile, and Beckett didn't miss the look exchanged by the Thorpes.

BECKETT WALKED ANDIE to her car as he did every evening after working on the window, but this evening she didn't want their time to end. Risking rejection, she glanced behind her. "What do you say to going and getting that drink now?"

"Drink?" Beckett at first looked cornered, but then his face relaxed. "Okay. But nowhere too crowded."

"I understand."

They met at a nearby twenty-four-hour diner, Lolly's. It wouldn't have been her first choice, but knowing Beckett's nervousness about crowds led her to choose this place. At ten in the evening, the diner tended to be quiet and almost empty.

The waitress seated them at a table near the back, and predictably Beckett took the spot that would enable him to keep his eyes on the front door. Andie supposed that his military training kicked in whether he wanted it to or not. Phoebe took her place under the table at Beckett's feet.

Andie accepted a menu from the waitress, but she didn't need one. Neither did Beckett it seemed since he placed his on top of hers and stared at her across the table. "This isn't quite the place I imagined when you asked me out for a drink that first night."

"I didn't ask you on a date that night. Not like you're thinking." She grinned and rearranged the cutlery in front of her. "I only wanted to get to know you better."

"Isn't that what dating is?"

Her answer was interrupted by the waitress who took their orders: a hot tea for Andie and a decaf coffee for Beckett. Plus, a piece of cherry pie with two forks.

Beckett gave a shrug to Andie after he ordered the pie and the waitress left to get their beverages. "No offense to Pattie, but I much prefer her other desserts to the fruit salad tonight."

"I think it's sweet how she looks after Russ."

"I'd say they look after each other."

Beckett kept his gaze on Andie, and she felt a flush rise up her chest. Now that their attraction for each other was out in the open, she felt as if she'd regressed to being an awkward teenager. She floundered to find a topic that didn't include the window or the Thorpes. Phoebe's head rested on Andie's knee, and she leaned down to scratch behind the dog's ears. "Phoebe seems to have settled in well with you."

"And me with her. Who knew that I'd take so quickly to a dog?"

"You didn't have dogs growing up?" In her mind, she could see a younger Beckett going off on adventures with his faithful pet.

He shook his head, then thanked the waitress as she set their drinks in front of them. "My dad was allergic to animals, so pets weren't a part of my childhood. I feel like I'm making up for it now with Phoebe."

"What does your dad say now?"

Beckett glanced away, and she regretted her question. When he turned back to her, his face had no emotion. "He died before my first tour in Iraq. My mom died when I was a teenager."

"I'm so sorry."

He paused for a long while. "It's been years since I've talked about family."

She couldn't imagine living her life without her mother and sister. "Do you have any family left?"

"A brother. Simon."

Before she could ask any more about it, he spoke in a tone that seemed too bright. "How is Cassie doing? Enjoying married life?"

In truth, she hadn't had much contact beyond a few texts and photos from her sister since the happy couple had left on their honeymoon. "I'm sure I'll hear all about it when they return next week from Venice."

Beckett raised an eyebrow. "Italian honeymoon? Nice."

"A wedding gift from the Buttucci brothers. They have family that's still there."

Once the waitress set the slice of pie between them, they ate and talked about other details of their daily lives. The house he was renovating. The doctor she worked for. The television show they'd last binge-watched. The small minutiae that normal people on dates might share.

And in that moment, it did feel normal. As if she might have a chance to pursue something with Beckett. And she really wanted to. Could think of little else as he paid for their dessert and walked her to her car in the parking lot. They stood silently facing each other before he made the first move.

The initial kiss she would describe as him testing the waters. To see if the heat they had experienced earlier had been a fluke. The second kiss confirmed that a fire flared when they touched. And the third kiss made her knees wobble and threaten to make her fall. But the tight grip that Beckett had on her meant she'd never fall.

She ended the kiss and took several deep breaths. "We should stop."

"Yes, we should."

Then he backed away as if to leave her, but she grabbed the front of his jacket and pulled him in closer. "Just one more."

One more kiss led to two more which ended in three. He pressed his forehead against hers after the last one. "You sure do know how to kiss."

"I could say the same about you."

"I like getting drinks with you, Andie, especially if they end like this." He kissed the underside of her jaw. "I'm looking forward to Saturday night. I'll pick you up at six."

She closed her eyes, reveling in the tingles that the kiss sent up and down her spine. "Saturday. Six."

She kissed him on the mouth once more, then told him good-night and got in her car. She knew that she'd be counting the minutes until their next date.

BECKETT PALED AT the crush of so many people packed inside the new restaurant. His buddy had assured him it was a soft opening, by invitation only. So why was there a crowd of people there? Aaron didn't know that many people, did he? Still, if his friend wanted the restaurant to succeed he would need a strong word of mouth and good press.

Andie sipped her glass of red wine and pointed to a less popular corner. "We could get some breathing room over there."

He appreciated that she could sense that the crowd raised his anxiety level. He nodded and took her hand, leading her to the quiet corner near the kitchen. Just below the din of the crowd, Beckett could hear the sharp orders from Aaron to his sous-chefs.

Andie leaned closer to him so he could hear her. "How do you know the owner?"

He swallowed as her nearness brought the scent of her perfume. "We served together in Iraq. He always claimed that once he got out of the army, he'd open up a restaurant."

"So this is his dream come true, then."

Beckett didn't share that Aaron's dream had been to marry his high school sweetheart who had sent a Dear John letter two months into his first tour. When the kitchen door opened, Beckett brought his arms around Andie to move her out of the way of a squad of waitstaff with trays of appetizers. The servers started to circulate in the crowd. A waiter handed plates of raw vegetables with various dips to him and Andie.

Andie plunged a carrot into one dip, nibbled the veggie and nodded with appreciation. "So all of Aaron's creations are vegan? From the size of this crowd and the good food, I'd say he will be a success."

Beckett used his pinky to dip into one

sauce and placed his finger in his mouth. Surprised to find the dip so tasty, he used a radish to taste more of it. They ate the appetizers, then sat down as the tasting plates offering different entrées were delivered to each table. Beckett had to squeeze closer to Andie to get a seat in the booth. Not that he minded being crushed to her side. She looked gorgeous tonight in a red dress that seemed to bring out the darker highlights in her hair. She reminded him of a chocolate-covered strawberry waiting to be tasted. And he wanted to be the only man to do just that.

Aaron walked out of the kitchen, and Beckett pointed him out to Andie as he greeted the guests. Eventually, his buddy got to their table. Beckett stood and embraced his brother in arms. "Congratulations. The food is amazing."

"Well, of course it is." He patted Beckett on the back and acknowledged Andie. "And who have we here?"

Andie stood and shook Aaron's hand as Beckett introduced them. "We've been working together on restoring a stained glass window."

Andie shot him a look. "That's not all we've been doing."

Aaron smirked at this, but Beckett chose to ignore it. Trying to describe his relationship with Andie wasn't easy.

"I've got to get back to the kitchen, Iceman, but I'm glad you came out tonight."

Andie frowned. "Iceman?"

"He hasn't told you that story?" Aaron slung an arm around his shoulder. "After our truck got firebombed and Ruggirello pulled him out of the flames, Beckett took down three snipers who'd been shooting at us from the rooftops. Didn't matter that his legs were still smoking from the flames. Ice in his veins. No emotions. Just pop. Pop. Pop. Dead."

Beckett shook his head. "It wasn't like that."

"I was there, buddy. It was exactly like that." Aaron turned back to Andie. "He saved our behinds that day because he kept his cool when everyone around him was losing their minds. Pushed our team to get in the truck behind ours and got us out. No casualties for our side." He patted

Beckett on the back. "Got a medal for it. Well deserved."

Andie looked at Beckett with a different light in her eyes, and he bristled at the change. He shot a hand out to Aaron and shook his, hoping to encourage his friend to leave them. "Well, congratulations on the restaurant. You deserve all the success."

Aaron gave them both a nod. "Thanks again for coming." Then he disappeared behind the kitchen door.

Beckett looked to Andie. "Are you ready to go?"

She frowned, likely not understanding the quick change of mood. What a minute ago seemed festive, now was not. The walls seemed closer than they had before, and the temperature of the room had risen to the point where he needed to remove his tie and suit jacket.

She mouthed, *Okay*, and he grasped her hand and pulled her through the crowd until they stood outside. He handed the valet the ticket for his truck, then pulled at his tie to loosen it and leaned against the restaurant's bay window. Placing a hand on his shoulder, she peered into his eyes. "Are you okay?"

He glanced around, was looking for possible threats. Scanning the roofs of the nearby businesses methodically until he realized that they were safe. He put a hand over his eyes. "Is it all right if we end our night early?"

ANDIE'S MOOD DIPPED with his words. She'd hoped that they could enjoy another date like a normal couple. She paused at that word. Would they ever be able to have a normal relationship? After this evening, she wasn't so sure.

Seeing Beckett's pained expression, Andie opened her purse and started pawing through it. "Do you have a headache? I can give you some aspirin?"

"Aspirin won't help."

She jerked back at the heat behind his words. "Why are you so angry?"

"Don't."

They'd been having a wonderful time, enjoying the food and the atmosphere. She'd even enjoyed getting a glimpse of who Beckett had been before she met him.

Aaron's words only confirmed what she'd always thought of Beckett—that he was a hero.

The valet pulled the truck to the curb, and Beckett opened the door to help Andie up into the vehicle before walking slowly around to the driver's side. It gave her time to think about what had changed. True, he'd had a moment of panic, but it had passed. He'd even laughed at something she'd said. She had thought they'd been able to get past his denial of being a hero, but it was obvious that Beckett still clung to the belief that he wasn't one. Why? Because he had killed people in order to save his own team? Did he think that would make her change her mind about him?

They drove in silence, and she snuck looks at him, trying to figure out what she could do to fix this. To make it better. If a friend of hers was in this situation, what advice would she give? Andie had a sinking feeling there was no answer.

When they arrived at her apartment, Beckett shut the truck off and they sat in silence for a moment. Andie could feel the distance starting to grow between them.

Longing for it to stop, she reached out and put her hand on his. He swallowed visibly, his ice-blue eyes full of a storm.

"Andie—"

"Don't say anything. Just kiss me." She leaned over and did just that. When they had kissed before, she could feel the Beckett she knew and loved responding to her. She hoped to find that man again.

But the moment passed, and she felt his lips tighten. He didn't have to tell her with words. She was losing him. Opening her eyes to stare into his, she could see the storm in them had settled into a resolute decision, and her heart seemed to still in her chest.

She scooted away from him, rested her head on the cushion and stared at the ceiling. What had she done that was so wrong? Why couldn't he love her?

When she turned to open the passenger door, she heard him say to her retreating back, "I'm sorry."

She turned to face him. "No, you're not. And I think that's what really hurts. Because you never wanted this to work."

"You don't understand."

"Then tell me."

He stared at her but didn't utter a word. "I can't do this anymore, Beckett. My heart can't handle this back and forth with you. Either you're with me or you're not." She raised her head to look at him. "And right now, you're not. So don't contact me. Don't invite me anywhere. And don't show up at my office with flowers. I'll be polite when we work on the window together. But when that's finished, so are we."

She hopped out of the truck and slammed the door behind her. She heard him get out of the other side and call her name, but she didn't turn back. She couldn't. If she did, she'd give in one more time. And Beckett would eventually back away, and she'd end up in the same position.

Cassie had been right. She was stuck in another nowhere relationship where she put in the effort only to be left alone in the end. Well, that stopped now. No more. Her heart couldn't take it.

She reached her apartment and quickly shut the door behind her, resting against it. She locked it tight to keep herself from running back to him. Instead, she put her hand on her chest. *I'm strong. I'm capable. I'm enough.*

CHAPTER THIRTEEN

ANDIE PLACED THE wrapped sheet of glass on the worktable. Using scissors, she carefully unwrapped the large square. "I think this will be perfect for the streams of light."

Beckett stopped cutting the glass at the other end of the table and barely acknowledged her or the glass before returning to his work. Russ stood closer and ran a hand over the surface. "It is perfect. Beckett?"

"I guess."

Russ leaned in closer to Andie and dropped the volume of his voice. "Someone's in a mood."

She really shouldn't care if Beckett was or not, but seeing him so distant and cold made her hurt even more than she had. She hitched the straps of her purse higher. "Well, I just wanted to drop that off. You both have a good night."

"You don't have to go." Russ turned to Beckett. "Ask her to stay."

She looked across the table at Beckett, but he stayed silent, his eyes focused on the cuts he made in the glass. With a hiccup, she left them and walked up the stairs.

She found Pattie in the kitchen, taking cookies off a baking sheet and placing them on a cooling rack. The older woman looked up and smiled at her. "Is it break time already?"

"I'm not staying."

Pattie frowned and placed the spatula on the counter. "Beckett looked glum when he got here."

"He doesn't want me here." She held up her hands in surrender. "He doesn't want me at all."

The words out of her mouth brought a fresh wave of tears. She startled when she felt Pattie wrapping her arms around her. "You go ahead and let it all out."

She immediately raised her head and took a step away from Pattie. "No. I'm done crying over him."

Pattie peered at her, not appearing to be

convinced by the words. She went and got a plastic container from a cupboard. "You take some of these cookies home."

"No, I couldn't."

"It's not much, but chocolate seems to ease a little of the heartbreak." She thrust the container into Andie's hands. "Before bed, eat two of these and add a big cup of tea. It will help you feel better in the morning."

Andie wrapped her arms around the container of cookies. "I know what you said about waiting for him, but I can't keep letting him break my heart."

"I know. A relationship like this isn't easy."

Not being easy didn't even begin to describe it. "I have to do what I think is best, right?" Still questioning if she was doing the smart thing, Andie looked at Pattie.

The older woman moved to the sink and stared out the window, an odd expression on her face. Was she recalling her own past experiences and how hard they'd been? "That's true. What's also true is that sometimes loving a warrior isn't for the weak willed."

"You think I'm weak?" The word made the ache in her chest swell. She was strong, wasn't she?

"No. You're not weak." Pattie shook her head. "You're just not ready."

"WHAT DID YOU do now?"

Beckett looked up from the glass he'd been cutting to see Russ's angry face. "Excuse me?"

Russ pointed to the ceiling. "That woman's been crying recently, and based on your mood, I'd say you're responsible." He glared at Beckett. "So what did you do?"

"Nothing."

That had been the problem. He couldn't give her what she wanted, so it was best for them both to let go. To give up their friendship.

Russ didn't look convinced. Instead, he made a noise in the back of his throat and exited the basement. Beckett brought his focus back to the cuts he needed to make. But his mind wandered to the woman who had left.

He'd be blind not to notice her tearstained

cheeks and reddened eyes. It had been several days since he'd last seen her, but he'd thought that she would be okay by now. But her appearance this evening had proven him wrong.

She wasn't fine just as he wasn't.

Andie had been right to tell him to leave her alone. As much as he might dream about her and wish to have a future with her, reality proved that they were better apart. But knowing it and accepting it were two different things.

She deserved so much more. While he might wish he could be the man to fulfill her dreams, he accepted his faults. Knew his failings. And being with Andie would only hurt them both.

Russ returned to the basement, glowering at him. "She's gone."

"It's probably better that way."

"You're such a fool."

Beckett stood and stared at the older man. "I'm trying to keep her from getting hurt worse later on."

"No, you think you're protecting yourself." He took a few steps closer. "I get it. I know your reasoning. But you're wrong."

He wished he was. If there was a chance for him to be with Andie, he would be running out of the house after her.

But there was no chance.

He went back to the glass as Russ muttered under his breath. "Let's just finish this pattern."

"You'll have to finish it another night."

Beckett raised his eyes to meet Russ's gaze. "You're kicking me out?"

"We've both lost our focus, so let's table this for now and get back to it in a few weeks."

"All of this because I won't date Andie?"

Russ shook his head. "Pattie and I are going on a cruise next week, and we'll be gone for ten days. I was going to tell you tonight." He stared at Beckett. "You need to take a step back from this and really think about what you want."

"I want to finish the window."

"You know what I mean."

Beckett rose to his feet. "I don't want Andie to get hurt."

"She already is hurting."

"Why can't everyone just leave me alone about this?"

Russ scowled at him. "You want to be alone? Fine. Go be alone. But when you finally realize that you need her, don't expect her to be there." Russ turned and started to walk up the stairs. "Or any of us."

Beckett struggled to accept the pain that his words had caused. Then he whistled softly to Phoebe. Russ was right. It was time for him to leave.

ENJOYING A RARE warm day in February at the park, Beckett threw the Frisbee for Phoebe to run after, applauding when she caught it in her mouth, then groaning as she dropped it and lay down on the damp grass. "You're supposed to bring it back to me."

He walked toward her and picked up the bright blue disc, petting the dog before straightening. "Want to try this again?"

Phoebe let out a sigh as if telling him that she was done chasing the Frisbee, but stood and waited for him to let it soar. She chased after it though let it drop and roll this time. This was obviously a work in progress.

His cell phone rang, and he glanced at the readout before answering it. He didn't recognize the area code, much less the phone number. He had a bad feeling about this call. "Beckett here."

"Lieutenant Beckett, this is Dr. Girard."

He searched his brain for any connection with a Dr. Girard. Finding none, he cleared his throat before asking, "I'm sorry, who?"

"Dr. Girard. I'm with Saint Anthony Hospital. You're listed as next of kin on my patient's records."

Next of kin. No, not another one. He closed his eyes and thought of his team members. "Who was it?"

"Private Christopher Lewis was brought to our emergency room a few hours ago. Attempted suicide."

Lewis had been green as a new blade of grass when he'd been assigned to Beckett's platoon on his last tour, but the time in Iraq had hardened the young man. While he'd been free with his smiles at the first, he'd returned without one of his legs or any of those grins. Beckett had meant to reach out to the young man to see how he was recuperating. *Please don't say it's been too late*. But the doctor had said "attempted." That meant he hadn't succeeded. So there was a chance. "Is he okay?"

"At the moment, he's still unconscious And it could be touch and go for the next few hours."

"Has his family been notified?"

"No family is listed. Just you."

The kid probably hadn't updated his records after returning from Iraq. Maybe Beckett hadn't reached out to him, but Lewis seemed to be asking for him to come. "When he wakes up, tell him I'm on my way."

Beckett hung up his phone and stared out at the patches of grass that peeked out underneath snow. The blades were brown, dead from the long absence of sun. Lewis had returned from war like that grass, and there were times Beckett felt the same. As if something inside him had died overseas.

And yet there'd been moments with Andie when he'd felt that piece of him stir, ready to grow and return to its former green glory. Those times thrilled him as much as they scared him. He'd allowed the fear to outweigh the excitement, and he'd turned her away for what he knew was the last time. She would one day become a dream of what might have been.

Ruggirello had allowed his fear and the darkness inside to take over his life until death became the only exit. And now Lewis had tried the same route. As much as Beckett might like to tell himself that he was stronger than the darkness, had his friends thought the same once?

Beckett whistled to Phoebe, and she retrieved the Frisbee before returning to his side. "Looks like we're going on a road trip."

THE ART GALLERY reminded her of a warehouse. Bare white walls. Concrete floors. She glanced around while she waited for the owner. Paintings wrapped in brown paper propped against the empty walls. Boxes and crates scattered around the large space. It had the feel of excited anticipation for something bigger and brighter.

"Andromeda, it's a pleasure."

She turned to see Keith Winchester coming up to her. It seemed he had lost what little remained of the hair on his head, since she had last met him, but his unlined face made him look younger than she knew he was. "It's been a long time."

He brushed off her words. "Not that long since we were in school. Or at least that's what I tell myself when I'm reminded of my age." He reached out and kissed both of her cheeks, then clasped both her hands in his. "I'm glad you could meet with me. What do you think of my new gallery?"

She made a sweeping glance of the open space. "It looks like it needs a lot more work."

He made a noise that mixed a groan with a laugh that didn't sound as if he was amused. "The grand opening is in a couple of weeks, and I keep finding more to do as the days go by. I could use an extra twelve hours in the day, but alas I'm only guaranteed the standard twenty-four."

He motioned for her to follow him to his office. Like the rest of the gallery, it too was in transition. His desk overflowed with papers and books while his bookcase stood empty. He pulled out a chair for her, then took a seat next to her. "Don't mind the mess. Once I hire a reception-ist, this will all be organized." He paused and looked at her. "How have you been?"

"Can't complain." She gave him a smile that she hoped was more confident than her tremulous nerves betrayed. "I see you're doing well for yourself. Your own gallery. That's amazing."

"I figured if I was going to really live my dream, then it had better be now." He reached over and touched one of her hands. "How is your father?"

"In prison, but then I'm sure you knew that."

"And your mother?"

"You've met Lillian, so you're familiar with her usual flair. To be honest, she's doing well, all things considered."

"That's good to hear."

"Speaking of mothers, how is yours?"

"You can see for yourself when you come to my grand opening. Daisy wouldn't miss it, and I hope neither will you."

Happy for her friend, she nodded. "I'll be here."

Keith steepled his fingers in front of his mouth and watched her for a moment. She wondered if he would finally tell her what this meeting was about. She'd spent most of last night wondering this very thing. Was he thinking of hiring her as his receptionist? Or maybe as a sales clerk. She could admit that the thought tempted her. To be surrounded by art every day. She might not be teaching, but it would get her closer to her own dream.

"Tell me, Andromeda, do you still create those wonderful glass sculptures like you did in college?"

She gave a laugh, shaking her head. "You remember those?"

"How could I not? You're very gifted."

It felt like she'd done that a million years ago. "I was. Not anymore."

Keith cocked his head to one side. "You gave up your art?"

"Real life intruded, and I needed to be practical and find a way to pay the bills." She folded her hands into her lap, hating how they trembled. "I changed my major to art education."

"So you're teaching, then?"

She almost winced at how her life had turned out. "I volunteer at the Community

Art Center twice a month, but I haven't yet been able to land a full-time teaching position in a school." But she would. She had to.

"Then my proposition comes at the right time." He leaned forward in his chair. "I want to sell your sculptures exclusively."

She backed away from him. Hadn't he been listening? "I told you, I don't make those anymore."

"Then don't you think it's time you start again?"

His words made her hands tremble even more. She shook her head at the foolish idea. She needed stability. A steady paycheck. Not the dream of creating art that meant something. "Reality is—"

"Highly overrated." He reached out and touched her hands, putting pressure on top of them to still them. "I've got studio space in the back where you can work. You'd divide your time between that and manning the sales floor with my other artists in residence." He looked her over with a speculative gleam. "What do you say?"

What could she say? Her heart might be interested, but her head reminded her that the starving artist life wasn't for her. "When do you need an answer?"

"Soon. What is your gut telling you?"

To sign the contract before he changed his mind. But her head kept telling her to get up and leave before he seduced her with promises that he wouldn't be able to keep. "Keith, I appreciate the offer, but—"

"You have a gift that is being wasted. You can't tell me no." He rose out of the chair and walked to the office door. "At least not until you see what I'm envisioning. Let me prove to you how I can make this work. And if you're still not convinced, I'll thank you for your time and see you at the gallery opening."

AFTER GETTING THE nurse's approval for Phoebe to accompany him to see the patient, Beckett entered the hospital room. PFC Lewis lay in the hospital bed, tubes and wires plugging him into various machines. A doctor glanced up at him before returning to her tablet and entering notes. The tag on her lab coat indicated that she'd been the one to call him. He reached Lewis's side and put his hand on the young man's arm. "Dr. Girard, I'm Laurence Beckett. I came as quick as I could. How's he doing?"

She gave a nod and returned to her notes. "The toxins in his system have been flushed out, but I don't yet know the extent of the damage to his nervous system. The next twelve hours are going to be critical."

Beckett kept his eyes on Lewis's still form as he took the young man's hand in his own. "Has his family been here yet?"

"Like I told you on the phone, he didn't have any family listed in his medical records. I believe you're the first and only visitor."

That surprised Beckett since Lewis came from a large extended family. He had expected to find at least his mother and an older sister or brother hovering over him. He squeezed Lewis's hand, but there was no response. Had Lewis pushed them away like Beckett had distanced himself from his own brother?

"Is there anything I can do?"

Dr. Girard clutched the tablet to her chest. "I think for now that he just needs to have your presence. He kept your name in his records for a reason, Lieutenant. So talk to him. Let him know you're here."

The doctor left them, pulling the curtain around them, and Beckett brought a chair closer to the bedside. Of all the soldiers under his care, Ruggirello might have been his best friend, but Lewis was like a kid brother. So young. So innocent. And so spirited. Beckett had kept an eye on him to make sure he didn't do something stupid that would get him or anyone else in their squad hurt or killed.

He should have called the kid. Should have made sure he was okay. But Beckett had pushed him away just like everyone else. He'd thought if he was alone, it would be easier. Safer.

Wasn't that why he'd let Andie go? Because if he let himself love her, she could be taken from him too. And losing her would be unbearable.

But he did love her. And still lost her all the same.

He quickly dismissed the thought. He couldn't let feelings for Andie intrude. Couldn't let himself travel down that impossible road.

He took a deep breath and scooted the chair closer to the bed. "Hey, Private. I'm here. So you can wake up anytime now."

No movement from the kid. Not that he'd expected a miraculous change, but still, he hoped. He reached over and put a hand on Lewis's shoulder. "I'll be right here, kid. I'm not leaving."

Phoebe looked up at Beckett, then settled on the floor beside the chair. They could be here awhile.

Beckett must have dozed off since the sound of alarms woke him. He stood as an army of nurses and doctors surrounded Lewis. One of them pointed at Beckett. "Sir, you'll have to step outside."

He stood rooted to the spot until she pushed at his arm. "Please, sir. We need the room to work."

He glanced at her, realized she was right and left the room. Phoebe followed him out into the hallway. Needing to do something, he paced, the dog matching his footsteps. He should have reached out. He should have checked in with the kid. He should have done more before this.

Please don't let him die.

Bands wrapped around Beckett's chest until he couldn't breathe. Placing his head in his hands, he leaned against the wall and slid to the floor. Phoebe nudged him. He couldn't breathe. Tightness. Shortness of breath. Pain everywhere.

He felt a hand on his shoulder. "Sir, are you okay?"

He couldn't speak. *Make it stop hurting. Make it go away.*

He heard a voice call for help, but it sounded so far away. The only thing that was close to him was the pain. And he feared that it wasn't going to go away this time. Despite everything he had done, it wouldn't end. No drugs. No therapy. No dog could touch this sorrow. Nothing could save him.

Voices surrounded him. A cool hand on his arm. "Sir, you seem to be having an anxiety attack. Concentrate on your breathing. That's better. Is there anyone we can call for you?"

Yes, maybe there was hope after all. Without a doubt, he couldn't do this on his own anymore. He needed someone to go through this with him. He pulled his cell phone from his pocket, and it fell from his hand. The nurse picked it up and gave it to him. "Take deep breaths, Lieutenant. You're going to be okay. And so's your friend. We think he's coming around."

He gave a nod to her, and she returned to Lewis's room. He took several deep breaths, concentrating as she had directed. In. Out. In. Out.

When he felt as if he'd regained control, he turned on the phone and pressed one of the auto dials. An answering machine picked up on the other end. "You've reached the Thorpe residence. Sorry we're not home right now—"

Right. They were on the cruise. He hung up and tried the next number. Andie's cell phone diverted straight to voice mail. He couldn't blame her for not taking his call. She'd asked him not to call her anymore. He didn't leave a message.

So alone. So isolated. It had been his choice. This had been what he wanted, right?

He'd been wrong. He needed people he loved in his life. Someone to help him through this darkness.

He squeezed his eyes shut and wished he had someone, anyone to talk to. He paused before dialing another number he hadn't called in years, wondering if he would answer after all this time. If the phone number was even still his. It rang three times before his brother answered, "Larry, is that you?"

Beckett paused, unsure if he was doing the right thing. But his brother had answered the phone rather than ignore the call, so maybe that was a good sign. Beckett tried to smile. "It's nice to hear your voice." His brother stayed quiet for a minute, and Beckett didn't know what to say. Had too much time passed? Was it too late? "I didn't know if you'd take my call."

"I wasn't sure either." A long silence, then a telling question. "What's wrong?"

Beckett put a hand on top of his head as he dipped it closer to his chest. "Where do you want me to start?"

Phoebe put her head in his lap as he laid out his troubles to his little brother.

AFTER THE TOUR of the studios with Keith and listening to his full proposal, Andie knew what she wanted to do. No, what she needed to do. All this time fixing other people's lives, it was time to fix her own. Time to pursue her own dreams and take a chance. Isn't that what she had wished for on New Year's Eve?

After signing the contract, she left the gallery feeling more herself than she had in a long time. She hadn't been this excited about her life since graduating college and looking toward a future ready to unfold in front of her. She pulled her cell phone out to call her sister with the good news. One missed call. Beckett. Why had he called her? She hadn't heard from him in two weeks, ever since he had made it clear that he wouldn't be in her life. And yet she knew if he had tried to reach her, it had to have been important. She hit the redial button.

When he answered, he sounded different. "Thank you for calling me back. I wasn't sure if you would after that night."

Wanting to set some boundaries and perhaps to protect her heart, she hardened her voice as she asked, "What's wrong? Has something happened?"

"This is going to sound crazy, but could you come to Toledo?"

She paused, unsure if she was ready to get pulled back into Beckett's orbit. What if he let her in only to push her way again? "Beckett, I told you that I can't keep doing this with you. This back and forth."

"I know what you said. But please come, Andie."

"Why?"

"Because I need you."

The words made her heart start to beat faster. He'd never said that to her before. If anything, he seemed to want to prove that he didn't need her at all. She didn't know how to answer his plea. "What for? You made it very clear that you don't want me around."

He let out a soft groan. "I was wrong, Andie. So wrong."

Andie thought of Pattie who had waited for years for Russ to come back to her. This could be her last chance with Beckett. While her heart might be urging her to agree to go see him, her head reminded her that she was already taking one chance with her art. Could she really afford to

take another one with Beckett? He seemed
to be waiting for her answer, but she didn't
know what she should say.

"Please, Andie."

"I can't always be at your beck and call
when you want me around. And then you
push me away. Again."

"That's not what this is. You're the one.
I know that now. Help me."

Her heart won out over her head. She
glanced at her watch. If she left now, she
could be there in two hours. "I'll see you
soon."

Had she made the right choice? Only
time would tell.

HOURS PASSED AFTER Beckett texted his location to Andie, sitting by the hospital bed
without a word from Lewis. A nurse came
to let him know that his brother had arrived.
Nerves made him pause before he left the
room. Had it really been six years since he'd
seen Simon? Maybe it was longer.

Would his brother be angry? Hurt? Yet
he'd come here at Beckett's request, so that
had to mean something. He took another
deep breath before he entered the waiting

room. Simon sat in a plastic chair near the window, slouched forward, elbows resting on his knees. When Beckett called his name, he looked up and gave him a smile.

Simon looked so much older than the last time he'd seen him, but one thing that hadn't changed was his brother's bone-crushing hug. "Larry, it's about time you called me."

"Sorry it's not under better circumstances."

They took a step away from each other, looking one another over and cataloging the changes that had occurred since they'd last been together. Then they hugged again, and Beckett held on to his little brother this time. "I shouldn't have cut you out of my life all these years."

"It's okay."

Beckett leaned back. "No, it's not. But I plan to make it up to you."

Simon gave a smirk that Beckett remembered very well. "Good. Because I don't intend on going anywhere. I don't care what you say."

The brothers sat in chairs, side by side. There was so much that Beckett wanted to say, but not near enough time to say it. "Again, thank you for coming down here."

"Has your friend woken up?"

Beckett shook his head. "Not yet, but the nurses say it should be soon. They think he's going to recover."

Simon patted his back. "That's good news, bro."

They talked a little more until a nurse entered the room and headed for Beckett. "He's waking up, sir. You might want to go back to his room."

Beckett stood. He wouldn't have minded taking his brother with him to see Lewis, but he had to do this on his own. "If you don't mind hanging out here for a bit, I have a friend, Andie, who's also driving down. I need someone to be here when she arrives."

"A girlfriend?"

Andie couldn't be described that way, but their complicated history would take too long to explain. "Be nice to her. And don't stare. She's quite the beauty."

When Beckett entered the hospital room, he found Lewis sitting up in the bed. The young man turned to look at him, blinking. "Lieutenant?"

Beckett walked over and stood next to the bed, a hand on the rail. "Private Lewis."

Lewis clawed at the tube stuck in his nose, but Beckett stopped him. "Don't do that. It's helping you get your oxygen level back up."

Lewis dropped his hands onto the bed. "Why are you here?"

"Because when one of my soldiers is in trouble, I want to be there."

Lewis's gaze landed on the blanket covering him. "Am I in trouble?"

Beckett looked steadily at the young man. "You tell me."

Lewis's eyes filled with tears, and he fumbled with the edge of the blanket. He took a deep breath. "It was just one thing after another, you know? I lost my leg, and the doctors put me on these painkillers which helped for a little while. But then they didn't. And I found if I chased them with a drink, it made me feel a whole lot better."

"Better?"

Lewis looked up at him. "Calmer. But then that meant I was showing up at work drunk, and you can guess how well that went over. They fired me before I could get things under control."

Beckett knew all about trying to control what was happening. He sat in the chair. "What about your family? I thought at least one of your siblings would be here by your side."

"We're not talking right now." Beckett listened as Lewis described how he'd rejected his family's many offers of help. "I couldn't let them see how much of a mess I was. They kept saying how I was a hero, but I didn't feel anything close to that. And then Jenny said she didn't want to go out anymore. That I had changed, and she didn't like the new me."

This kid's story could have been his own if he had given up on himself. If he'd rejected the people around him. But Beckett hoped that he was now getting a second chance. The same as Lewis.

"Losing my girlfriend was the last straw, you know? Felt like I couldn't do anything right, so I thought why not just

stop doing everything. Stop the nightmares. Stop the anxiety attacks. Stop all
of it. I heard about how Spatz, Miller and
Ruggirello died. Three good guys, and
they're gone. And I thought I'd just be
one more."

Lewis kept his eyes down, as if afraid
to see how Beckett would react. But he
couldn't judge the young man for grap-
pling with the same thoughts he'd had.
Beckett scooted to the edge of the chair.
"And what do you think now?"

"I don't want to die."

The words came out softly, but they
were said. Beckett believed him. He gave
a short nod. "Good. I don't feel like going
to any more of my friends' funerals."

Lewis looked up at him, tears tracking
down the kid's cheeks. "But I don't know
where to go from here. What am I going
to do?"

"How about you take it one day at a
time for now?" Beckett reached over and
put his hand on the young man's. "And
what if you think about coming to work
for me in Michigan?"

The young man had a ghost of a smile. "And take orders from you again?"

"You have better plans?"

Lewis met his gaze and shook his head. "No, sir."

THE WAITING ROOM at the hospital had several groups of people congregating. Andie scanned the faces until she found a younger version of Beckett reading a magazine, Phoebe at his feet. She approached the dog and crouched down to put her hand in the thick fur. "Hey, girl. Where's your owner?"

"You must be Andie."

She looked up at the speaker. "And you must be Beckett's brother. You have the same eyes."

He thrust his hand toward her. "Simon."

"Where is he?" She glanced around the room once more, but knew that he wasn't there.

"Visiting with his friend."

Andie took a seat next to Beckett's brother. "I was shocked to get his call."

"No more than I was. I haven't heard from him in six years, then out of the blue,

I get a phone call from him?" Simon gave a low whistle. "I knew he must be in trouble if he was calling me."

"Is he in trouble?"

Simon turned to look at her. "I think we're both here to help him stay out of it." He smiled so much like Beckett it made Andie's heart long for him. "You know, he told me you were beautiful, but like usual he didn't do you justice."

"Are you hitting on my girl?" Beckett stood a few feet from them.

Simon held his hands up. "Just repeating what you told me."

Andie peered at Beckett. He looked different. Less burdened, in a sense. A weight taken off him. She stayed sitting, waiting to see if he would come to her. After all, he'd said he needed her. And she'd driven two hours to be here. He had to take these last few steps. Had to come to her first before she would let him back in.

He gazed back at her. "Andie."

But he stayed standing where he was. Slowly, she stood and that seemed to be all the encouragement he needed. He rushed forward and pulled her into his arms.

Pressing kisses into her hair. "Thank you for coming."

She took a step back from him, and he dropped his hands, then glanced behind her at his brother. "We'll be back. Do you want something to drink, Simon?"

"I'll take something cold and sweet."

Beckett took her hand and they left the waiting room. "Where are we going?" she asked, still unsure if this was the right thing to do.

"Somewhere with less prying eyes."

"Why?"

He stopped to face her. "So I can kiss you without an audience."

She dropped his hand. His expression seemed to be questioning her. "So I'm just supposed to let you back in as if nothing has happened? Forget the tears and heartache? Then what? You change your mind, and I'm alone again."

She couldn't give in so easily. Pattie might have let Russ come back, but Andie wasn't Pattie. She had her own journey, one she'd hoped would include this man. But hadn't he made it clear that he couldn't be with her?

"I know I've hurt you, Andie. I'm sorry."

"Those are just words. You've said them before."

He blew out a breath and ran a hand through his hair. His gaze was stricken. "What do you want from me?"

She'd thought of her answer the entire car ride to Ohio. "You. All of you. Even the parts that you're scared of."

He stared at her for a long moment. She had lost him again. She could see the panic fighting with another emotion. Love? She hoped it was, but she didn't know which would win. And she couldn't wait around for him to make up his mind. *I'm strong. I'm capable. I'm enough.*

She held up a hand. "I'm glad you're okay, but I don't think I need to be here after all."

Turning on her heel and calling herself all sorts of names for hoping to believe it would be different this time, she started to walk away. But Beckett reached out and grabbed her hand. She turned to look at it and at him. He caressed her hand with his thumb, the calluses sending shivers up her spine. "You're wrong. I do need you."

"For what?" Again, he didn't say a word. She reached up and put her left hand on the side of his face. "Tell me or I walk away for good."

He glanced around them. Nurses, doctors, patients, families walked alongside them in the hallway though barely looking at them. He turned back to her, taking a step closer. So close that she could feel the heat coming off his body. He peered into her eyes and framed her face with his hands. "I don't want to be alone."

"You could have any woman. Why me?"

He groaned and tipped his head back, staring at the ceiling. "You know I'm not good with words, Andie."

She wasn't going to give in. He had to say the words. Had to prove that he was in it for the long haul this time. She admired Pattie for her determination and patience, but Andie couldn't wait years for Beckett to be ready.

It was now or never.

CHAPTER FOURTEEN

LOOKING INTO HER EYES, which shone with wariness, Beckett knew this was going to be his last chance with Andie. He had hurt her before, but he'd realized that he needed her in his life. And not as a friend. He wanted to be her everything. She waited for the words. Deserved them. But he didn't know how to tell her.

She put her hand on his, then pulled them away from her. "Tell me, Beckett."

As he'd waited for Lewis to wake up, he'd thought about what he would say to Andic. And now that she was here, he couldn't think of the speech he'd been rehearsing. She deserved to hear what was in his heart, so he took a deep breath. "I know I don't deserve you. You should have a man who doesn't come with my baggage. I'm damaged, and I don't know if I can ever be completely healed. But I'm trying. And I'm all the better for knowing you."

He reached out and touched the ends of her hair that lay on her shoulder. "You make the scary parts inside me disappear. It's like I'm not the man I once was, but someone I want to be. For you, I could almost be that hero you're always talking about."

She smiled the warmest smile he'd ever laid eyes on. "You are my hero. Eventually, you will see the man you are when you look in the mirror. In the meantime, I'll remind you every day that you are a good and honorable man."

He put his arms around her, wanting to crush her to him and never let go. "Don't give up on me, Andie. I love you, and I don't think I can let you go again."

"Then don't ever let go. No matter what."

She reached up to press her mouth to his. He put his hands on her hips and pulled her closer, wrapping her tighter to him.

He wasn't going to let her go. He would hold on to her during the good times but especially the bad. He didn't want to face a future without her.

When he released her, he couldn't stop touching her. He held one of her hands as they found a vending machine down the hall. He retrieved the coins from his jeans pocket one-handed and put them in the machine.

Returning to the visiting room with the three drinks, they took seats next to his brother, but Beckett put his arm along the back of her chair, his hand buried in her hair. He knew that he didn't deserve this third chance with her, much like he didn't deserve the woman herself. He also knew that they had challenges ahead of them, but as long as she was by his side, he could face anything.

LATER THAT EVENING, Simon stretched on one of the beds in the motel room near the hospital. Beckett had hoped to have Andie to himself, but it had been good to spend this time catching up with his brother. Simon planned on returning home the next day, but Beckett knew that it wouldn't be years before they talked again. He was going to fix this relationship too.

Beckett turned to Andie and she pointed behind her shoulder. "I'll just go to my room. It's late, and I should let you both get some sleep."

"I'll walk you to your door." Beckett rose.

She put a hand on his shoulder. "That's sweet, but you don't have to. I'm just across the hall."

Beckett couldn't help but grin, after a glance at his brother. "I want to."

He told Simon he'd be back in a moment, then walked her across the hall and waited as she unlocked the door to her room. When she started to walk through, he slipped his hand in hers, not wanting to say good-night just yet. She turned to look at him. "What is it?"

"It's good to have you here, Andie. After everything that's happened with us, I'd understand if things had gone differently." He reached out and tucked a stray curl behind one ear. "There's so much more I want to say to you."

"I'm listening."

He took a deep breath. "When I look at Lewis, I see where I might have wound up. What I might have done if I had kept pushing everyone away. Pushing you away." He touched her cheek. "But I'm done with that. I've discovered that I can't do this alone. And more important, I don't want to. What I want is a family and friends, and especially, you, Andie. With you, I feel safe."

Andie looked at him, a tender expression on her face. "And with you, I feel more alive."

He stared into her eyes, hoping he could communicate everything he was feeling. It was a little overwhelming. "I can't promise that things will always be easy. The anxiety attacks aren't going to disappear as if by magic. And the dark moods might pop up now and then. But what I can promise is that when I'm afraid, I won't push you away. I'll hold out my hand."

"And I'll be there to take it." She squeezed his hand. "Together, we'll get through this. No matter what."

"No matter what."

He leaned in and pressed his lips to hers. Their kiss earlier might have been a start, but this one was like finally coming home. No more questions. No more back and forth. No more doubts. Just a man and a woman fitting all their pieces together so that nothing could break them apart again.

ANDIE HANDED HER purse over to the prison guard to be searched before she followed her sister into the waiting room. Usually it was Cassie who suggested that they visit their father, but Andie had been the one to suggest it this time. She needed to see him after everything that had happened between her and Beckett. Because maybe Cassie was right about her issues with their dad.

Cassie nudged her as they took seats in the metal chairs. "Are you okay? You were pretty quiet on our drive here."

How could she describe how much better she felt? Some of it was taking the job at the gallery, but resolving the relationship between her and Beckett had set her emotions soaring. She felt free. Hopeful about an amazing future just waiting for her, but first she had to tie up the past. And that meant being here, talking to her father.

Not to get his approval on any of the decisions she'd made recently. She'd waited too long already for him to give it to her, and now she understood she no longer needed it. No, this was about her taking back the power he seemed to have over her.

She glanced at Cassie and nodded. "I'll be better once this is over."

Her sister raised an eyebrow at her words. "What's going to be over? What are you expecting to happen today?"

Andie didn't get to answer since their father entered the room. He looked even more stooped and doughy than he had the previous month. When he took a seat across the table from them, he didn't say a word or have a glimpse at them. Just kept his head down.

"Hi, Daddy." Cassie couldn't seem to let the silence continue. "You look…" Her voice trailed off. "How are you doing?"

He shook his head, but kept his gaze on

the table. Andie felt a twinge of sympathy. "What's wrong, Daddy? Why can't you look at us?"

He raised his head and glared at Andie. "You shouldn't have come here."

Cassie gasped. "Daddy, we wanted to see you."

"Why? So you can go home and feel better about your pathetic lives while your father rots in jail?" He lifted his hands and set them on the table.

"And whose fault is it that you're here?" Andie sat up straighter in her chair. He was acting like he was the victim here? No, no. Not on her watch. "And we don't have pathetic lives. Cassie brought pictures from her wedding for you to see. And I just got a good job at a new art gallery."

Her father glowered at her. "Goody for you. I'm so glad to hear that you two get to move on."

Cassie started to huff, but Andie put her hand on her sister's as if to protect her from their father's words. "Yes, we're moving on, and it's a good thing too. You might have to stay in prison, but Mother,

Cassie and I had to deal with the fallout of your crimes. We're finally coming out from under the cloud that your conviction created over all of us."

"I didn't—"

Andie stood and stared down at her father. "I'm not finished talking. I can't speak for Cassie, but I am done trying to live up to your impossible standards. Standards that even you couldn't live up to, by the way." She paused, not wanting to let her father see the tears that threatened. She cleared her throat. "It's time for me to live my own life pursuing my dreams. I've finally found my perfect job and a man who loves me for who I am. And if you can't be happy for me, then I won't be coming back."

Cassie rose to her feet and clasped her wedding photo album to her chest. "And I won't visit either."

Their father glanced between them. "You want me to cry now? Boo-hoo because you won't see me? I didn't want you to come here in the first place."

He rose to his feet and walked away from the table. Cassie glanced at Andie as if she were seeing her for the first time. "You were awesome. You didn't back down or anything."

"It didn't work though, did it? He left us." She watched as the door closed behind her father and felt the first tear fall from the corner of her eye.

"But that's on him, not us." Cassie reached over and grabbed her hand, squeezing it. "You've changed, Andie."

"I won't let him treat me like I'm nothing anymore. I'm strong. I'm capable. And I'm enough just as I am."

"But that's the thing. You always were."

Andie gave her a soft smile. "But I finally believe it now."

WITH RUSS AND Pattie back from their cruise, Andie's nights were once again dedicated to repairing the window. The pattern of the window had been filled in with the various pieces of glass, and was ready to have its border wrapped in lead before being soldered together.

Across the worktable, Russ held up a piece of border for Beckett to see. "This groove in the middle of the lead will be your guide to wrapping the glass." He picked up a piece that would be attached to the border and demonstrated. "See?"

Andie cradled her wrist still in the cast. She had another week until she could have it removed, but she was tempted to find a saw in Russ's basement and do the honors herself. Her skin itched like crazy, and she wanted to be able to help more with the window.

Now that they were on the lead stage, it would go faster. Depending on their busy schedules, they could finish it within the month. She couldn't wait to see it installed at the house Beckett had been renovating.

She also couldn't wait to share the news she had been sitting on. She cleared her throat, and the two men stopped wrapping glass to look up at her. "I found the window's artist."

Russ plopped down on his stool, and waited for her to continue, while Beckett stood still, watching her. "Well?" Beckett asked.

"His name was William Casper. He made about a dozen stained glass windows in the early 1920s, but only four that they know about remain." She nodded at the pieces of glass before them. "Five now, including this one."

Beckett's jaw had dropped. "Who was he?"

"He was primarily a local artist. I couldn't find out a lot about him, but what I did find out would interest you both." She paused as she looked at them. "He served in the trenches in France during World War I and returned to the States suffering from shell shock."

Russ nodded. "A different term for PTSD."

"My professor found some letters in an archive that describe how he used working with glass to help him with the dark thoughts that followed him home from war." She reached out and touched one of the pieces of glass. Should she share the rest of Casper's story if it could hurt the two men that she cared about? But she'd come this far, and the truth always had a way of revealing itself. "He died before he turned thirty which is why there aren't more windows."

Beckett stiffened. "Suicide?"

"No. A car accident. But he never married or had children. He died alone." She looked up at Beckett and kept her eyes on him. "His letters to his sister describe how making the stained glass windows helped to make him feel whole again. He said that he put lighthouses in all his windows because they represented a safe harbor. Art helped to save him from the horrors he'd experienced."

Beckett swallowed and closed his eyes as Russ gave a low whistle. "No wonder we connected to this window. The artist was just like us."

"No, not like us." Beckett opened his eyes and looked across the table at her. "We're not alone, and we won't be. We've got each other, right?"

"Right."

They returned to work, the mood more somber than it had been before she'd shared her news. Andie looked over the pattern and groaned at the sight of one of the pieces of glass in the lighthouse that had a tiny crack. "We've been so careful, and now this? We're out of the red glass.

That means we have to recut this entire section with new glass in another color."

Beckett reached out and stilled her hand when she started to remove the red pieces. "No, let's keep it that way."

"But it's cracked. Flawed."

He nodded. "It doesn't have to be perfect to be beautiful. I'm learning that even the scars or imperfections have their own appeal."

His words warmed her heart. She clasped his fingers and nodded. "It's accepting the scars that bring something beautiful out of what might have otherwise been thrown away."

Neither one of them would ever be tossed aside because they weren't perfect. They had each other.

When they finished for the evening, Pattie brought out a chocolate torte for them all. "You don't know how much I've missed our evenings together. I enjoyed going on the cruise, but I love baking for you all even more."

The older couple took turns sharing stories from the cruise. When the last bite was eaten, Russ peered at Beckett and then Andie. "That's what we've been up to. What about the two of you?"

Andie shrugged. "I gave my two weeks' notice at the doctor's office."

Pattie gasped. "You got a teaching job."

"Actually, I'll be working at an art gallery part-time." She took a sip of her tea. "I'll have a studio there and for the rest of my time, I'll be creating glass sculptures."

Russ clapped his hands. "It's great that you've returned to your artistic roots. I'd like to think I had a hand in that by insisting you fix the window." He redirected his attention to Beckett. "But that's not what I was referring to."

Andie could feel her cheeks grow hot as Beckett reached across the table and took her hand in his. Pattie beamed at the two of them as Russ hit his fist on the table. "I knew it. I could have said you two would end up together that first night you walked in here."

"We're still in the early days of this and trying to figure out what our future will look like." Beckett rubbed his thumb across hers. "But I know that I've never had someone like Andie before. And I'm not letting her go again."

"Andromeda in Greek mythology was saved by a hero." Russ glanced between them both. "But tell me, Beckett, did our Andie save you?"

Beckett squeezed her hand and shook his head. "I think we saved each other."

BECKETT'S HOUSE HAD never had so many people inside it. He'd intended to hold the party in the backyard, but a week of early-May rainstorms had turned it into a mud pit that Phoebe loved to roll around in. He only hoped everyone he'd invited would fit inside. He'd never been good with a crowd, but a night like this deserved to be celebrated with family and friends.

Andie took over his kitchen, directing people where to get food and drinks as he answered the front door and welcomed his guests. Russ walked up behind him, a red plastic cup of pop in one hand. "You're lucky to have her, you know."

He gave the older man a nod. "I'm lucky to have you too. I don't know what

I would have done if you hadn't agreed to work on the window with us."

Russ didn't say anything, but the older man's eyes glistened as he patted Beckett on the back before joining his wife. Pattie was speaking with Andie's mother. Lillian seemed to have accepted him, albeit begrudgingly. She'd taken him aside a few weeks ago and threatened to harm him if he ever hurt her daughter. He'd promised to do everything in his power to keep that from happening. Then he'd gotten a visit from the Buttucci brothers who issued the same warning.

The doorbell rang again, and Beckett welcomed Lewis. The young man looked as if he was starting to gain back some weight and had a healthier glow than when he'd been in the hospital almost three months before. Working with Rob and Beckett seemed to have given the young man purpose, and with the help of a few others, while he wasn't completely out of the woods, he was well on his way to recovery. "Glad you could make it."

"Kind of hard to refuse when the boss invites you," the kid teased.

Lewis paused and glanced at all the people. He took a step back, but Beckett patted him on the shoulder. "It's okay. You're safe here."

The young man looked up at him, then took a tentative step forward. "Think I'll go get a drink." He glanced at Beckett. "Pop. Not alcohol."

Lewis would be okay. Beckett would keep an eye on the young man to make sure of it. Maybe the two of them could figure it out together. Lewis had reached out to his family, but they were understandably hesitant while he was still in his recovery. But the first step had been taken.

Beckett had even begun bringing Rob and Lewis to the monthly meetings with Russ's vet friends. He never expected to find comrades in arms across so many battlefields, but there it was. They knew. They understood. And they helped him find answers when there didn't seem to be any.

Another knock on the door, and Beckett turned to welcome more to the party. His brother stood on the doorstep holding hands with a young woman. The journey back to being family hadn't been easy, but they were taking it together. "You're late."

"You said seven. I'm right on time."

"Early is on time. And on time is—"

"Late," they finished saying together.

He grabbed his brother in a tight hug before Simon had the chance to say another word. Beckett had learned his lesson, and he wasn't going to let his own family get away from him again.

His brother laughed, but returned the hug. "Easy, bro. Or you're going to embarrass me in front of my date."

"Too late. You're already an embarrassment," Beckett said before releasing his brother and letting him introduce the woman beside him.

Once everyone had arrived, Beckett called Andie up to the front of the group where an easel was draped with a white sheet. He put his arm around her waist and turned to their family and friends. "On New Year's Eve, I found what I thought was a treasure. A stained glass window that was hidden behind a wall. Cracked and broken, it looked a lot like I felt.

"I sent out a call for help, and this angel right here answered." He turned to Andie, who pinked at his words. "She told me she couldn't fix it, but she knew someone who could." He pointed to Russ, who clasped his hands and held them above his head like a victor. "Russ said he'd teach us, and together we brought back something that was discarded.

"Turns out the artist of this window was a vet returning from World War I. He had scars and nightmares of his own, but creating the window helped restore him. I know the feeling because repairing it brought healing for me. So tonight, I'm proud to show you the window, restored to its former glory."

Together, Andie and Beckett removed the sheet to reveal the window. People gasped and exclaimed at the reveal, taking turns to walk up and get a better look.

Cassie walked up to Beckett when he had a moment alone. She looked over at her sister who talked with his brother, Simon. "I've never seen her glowing like that. I think that's because of you."

He hoped it was. "Love will do that."

"I could say the same for you. You don't look as restless as you once did."

Love had done that too. He didn't need to be afraid of the future anymore. Not with Andie by his side. "I know I don't deserve Andie, but I will try every day to be better for her."

"I think you're both good for each other, but then I guess that's what you look for in a partner." She glanced across the room, and he saw her smile at her husband, who gave her a wink. "Welcome to the family."

It was as if she knew about the ring that waited in his top dresser drawer as soon as he had the perfect moment. He gave a short nod. "Thank you, Cass."

Later, with everyone gone, Andie and Beckett stood in front of the window, their arms around each other's waists. So much work had gone into it, and now it was ready for its new home, here in Beckett's house.

Andie rested her head on his shoulder. "Are you certain you want to hang it here instead of maybe selling it?"

He placed a hand on her cheek. "Why would I want to give away something so beautiful? That has come to mean so much to me?"

"You'll keep it no matter what?"

He placed a soft kiss on her lips, knowing they weren't talking about the window anymore. "No matter what."

* * * * *

For more great
Harlequin Heartwarming romances,
please visit www.Harlequin.com today!

ReaderService.com has a new look!

We have refreshed our website and
we want to share our new look with you.
Head over to ReaderService.com
and check it out!

On ReaderService.com, you can:

- Try 2 free books from any series
- Access risk-free special offers
- View your account history & manage payments
- Browse the latest Bonus Bucks catalog